PORTFOLIO
BRAND SHASTRA

Mainak Dhar is an alumnus of the Indian Institute of Management, Ahmedabad, and has spent over two decades in the corporate sector. He began his career with Procter & Gamble, spending close to eighteen years there in marketing and general management roles in India and across the Asia–Pacific region. In early 2014, after fifteen years abroad, he moved back as the CEO of the India operations of a major multinational consumer products company. A self-described cubicle-dweller by day and writer by night, Mainak is also the author of over a dozen books, some of which have been bestsellers and have been translated into several languages. When he's not at work or spending time with his wife, Puja, and son, Aaditya, he can usually be found thinking of, or working on, his next book. Learn more about him and contact him at www.facebook.com/AuthorMainakDhar.

BRAND SHASTRA

USE THE POWER OF MARKETING TO TRANSFORM YOUR LIFE

MAINAK DHAR

PORTFOLIO
PENGUIN

An imprint of Penguin Random House

PORTFOLIO

USA | Canada | UK | Ireland | Australia
New Zealand | India | South Africa | China | Singapore

Portfolio is part of the Penguin Random House group of companies
whose addresses can be found at global.penguinrandomhouse.com

Published by Penguin Random House India Pvt. Ltd
4th Floor, Capital Tower 1, MG Road,
Gurugram 122 002, Haryana, India

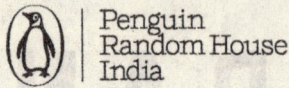

Penguin Books Ltd, Registered Offices:
80 Strand, London WC2R 0RL, England
For more information about the Penguin Group visit penguin.com

First published in Portfolio by Penguin Books India 2016

Copyright © Mainak Dhar 2016
Illustrations copyright © Priyankar Gupta 2016

The views and opinions expressed in this book are the author's own and the facts
are as reported by him, which have been verified to the extent possible, and the
publishers are not in any way liable for the same.

ISBN 9780143425700

Typeset in Adobe Caslon Pro by Manipal Digital Systems, Manipal
Printed at Manipal Technologies Limited, India

As always,
for Puja and Aaditya

Contents

Preface

From time immemorial when Adam was tempted to reach for the apple on the Tree of Knowledge to a more-present time when we are swayed by 140-character exhortations on social media to vote for one party over another, a particular power has been exerting its influence on how we make choices in our lives. The answer may surprise you.

That power is marketing.

Not the sort of marketing you'd expect to study in business school, but marketing as a set of postulations, in its core essence, as the study of human behaviour and perceptions and how to influence them. All of us intuitively understand and wield the power of marketing every day, whether we realize it or not. *Brand Shastra* distils some of the core principles of marketing and shows how their application in everyday situations can help each of us make every single day of our lives a little bit better. From losing weight to executing a better work–life balance to how we incentivize the right behaviour in our children, there are lessons and insights in this book that you'll find yourself relating to and applying in all aspects of how you lead your life.

That connection is what has made me love my career in the consumer products industry and has kept me energized

and eager to learn even after twenty years. It has meant
that my work, while indeed being about building brands
and businesses, helps me understand how people think and
work, and in turn helps me become a better person. At a
very personal level, marketing for me is about using an
understanding of others to make ourselves more empathetic,
more effective and have a more positive impact on those
around us.

That was what motivated me to write this book,
because I want to show how applying some basic concepts
of marketing can help us understand the world around us
better, and perhaps influence it to meet our needs. You don't
need to be a marketer or student of marketing to read this.
Indeed, I suspect you'll enjoy it more if you aren't burdened
with concepts and theories. All you need is an open mind
and curiosity to see how the world around us isn't all
happenstance and destiny, how so many of our choices are
shaped by marketing and how, by being plugged into that,
you can retake control of some of those reins.

Combining the business and branding experience of a
CEO with the storytelling ability of a novelist, I have tried to
craft *Brand Shastra* as a unique book that will stimulate and
inspire you to make those connections of your own.

1

Adam's Apple to Acche Din

A Brief History of Marketing

In the beginning, there was lack of awareness.

That's probably not how you've heard the beginning of human history described. But in many ways one could argue that is how it all began. All of us know the story of Adam and Eve, placed in the idyllic, uncorrupted Garden of Eden by God. They were free to do all they wanted, other than of course sample the fruit from the Tree of Knowledge. Then came the first marketer of them all—Satan—and he did what great marketers have done ever since then: Make what has been in front of us seem suddenly desirable. In this case, from Adam's point of view, both the apple and Eve.

And so the apple that had been there all along suddenly became not just any apple, but the Forbidden Fruit. It was a feat of branding that would make many modern marketers proud.

So awareness turned to desire, and desire to 'trial'.

The rest, as they say, is history. Our history; one where we have been made to desire or loathe things, to reject or accept trends, based on how our perceptions towards them have been shaped and influenced. It is through that long history of marketing that the thread of our civilization has been woven. In case you're wondering where marketing fits into all this, let's step back a bit and understand what marketing really is.

When I was in business school at the Indian Institute of Management, Ahmedabad, more than two decades ago, being introduced to marketing through case studies and textbooks, I might have been forgiven for thinking that marketing was all about constructs and theories, things academicians wrote books about and whose application was limited to the world of business. Since then I have spent two decades on the front lines of marketing and general management in consumer product companies. This experience has made me realize that marketing is both much simpler and infinitely more complicated. It is simpler because, at its core, marketing has very little to do with theories and formulas. Marketing is about something each and every one of us can relate to and understand—human perceptions, motivations and behaviour. From a child who fakes a tantrum to get what he wants, to a young man who professes his undying real love to get the object of his affection into bed, to the employer who comes up with different employee-engagement programmes to get employees to be more loyal and committed, we are all wired to understand people's motivations and how to influence their behaviour to meet our needs.

That understanding and shaping of people's perceptions and behaviour, after all, is what any marketer does, whether it's making you feel a bottle of sugar-filled soda somehow represents your youthfulness or whether your mobile phone being represented by a half-eaten fruit or a rotund robot represents the kind of person you are. When I say marketing is infinitely more complicated, it is because there is perhaps nothing more difficult to understand than human motivations and needs. We are fickle, we change, and what we find desirable today becomes old news tomorrow. That's why professional marketers spend years and millions in research funding trying to understand consumers and understanding how to structure approaches to winning over these consumers. That is also perhaps why I love marketing. It's not just about solving problems in the world of business, but instead it's about the here and now, about everyday people making everyday choices. I've found that understanding the broad concepts of marketing, such as how to position and promote a brand, can unlock something incredibly valuable, much more satisfying than just selling a brand or product. It brings us closer to understanding people—an understanding of how perceptions, memories and behaviour intersect to drive so many of our day-to-day life choices and help us relate to those around us.

It's also about inspiring, about making people reach for things that they might have considered unreachable. Indeed, much of human history has been about great marketing making people stretch and leap forward. There has been the darker side of marketing as well, propagating hatred and prejudice, but then progress and prejudice are both part and parcel of human nature. It's what side of human nature we want to appeal to that determines the role marketing plays, for marketing at the end of the day, is a tool, to be used as you want. If you think I'm overstating the role marketing has played in history, consider some well-known examples that may make you reconsider your stand.

Thousands of years ago, a civilization came up and thrived in what today is western India. We know of its existence from the ruins and artefacts left behind in ancient cities like Mohenjo-daro and Harappa. The seals left behind have been studied by academics who linked them with Hindu gods. They hypothesized these as links to the religions and cultures that followed in India. Historians and archaeologists marvel at how well planned these cities were and how such a civilization took root and spread across a huge geography, in some cases even before the birth and dissemination of a systematic language code. But they puzzle over how these flourishing civilizations came to a sudden end.

Very few people recognize that the Indus Valley Civilization was perhaps home to the world's first multinational consumer products enterprise. This enterprise created 'branded' products which were sold to consumers in faraway lands. Many scientists today believe that the seals served more than an ornamental or religious purpose, but served to trademark the products from particular artisans or villages. (More on that in the coming chapter.) When we talk about 'Make in India' today, we should not be thinking of it as a new concept. This concept is connected with the seeds that were forged in the workshops of Mohenjo-daro, Harappa and Lothal. Here the first truly global marketers were embarking on launching their products into new markets overseas. Their manufacturers were facing and solving problems of how to brand products to make them stand out, which we are mistakenly taught (especially in marketing schools) were first cracked by modern consumer product companies and their marketers armed with MBA degrees. Yes, India was perhaps the progenitor of branding.

So let us carry the story on to see how what we think are modern marketing concepts are actually so intrinsic to human behaviour that they have been in play since the dawn of ancient civilizations.

Fast forward a couple of 1000 years, and we come upon an emperor who struggled with a problem that modern marketers confront every day: You have your message ready and you think your message is the right one to get the desired impact among your target audience. Now, how do you get the message out to your target audience in the most effective manner? That is a critical issue to solve because while you may have the best possible message, if it does not reach your desired target audience, it really doesn't matter. Ashoka, the emperor in question, more than 2000 years ago, did not have media planners to help him find a solution to his dissemination problems. But what he did have was an intuitive knowledge of his 'consumers'. He came up with an excellent solution to get his message across to his people. He ensured it reached not just the most numbers, but when his audience was also receptive to his message.

Ashoka put up his messages about law and society on pillars and carvings spread across much of now modern India, Bangladesh and Nepal. What he had done was a spark of genius. He had placed these pillars near important trading routes. In those days, without TV or the Internet to reach people in their homes, most news of the outside world came from travellers on these routes. This was the equivalent of a modern marketer advertising on popular Facebook pages, reaching their consumer where there is high traffic and 'engagement'. With this one stroke, Ashoka ensured his messages reached the millions of people who lived in his empire. This played a major role to unify these people through ideas, unlike other rulers, who used the sword or taxes. Other rulers may have had similar thoughts on unifying their people, but for them, that message was carried down through a series of intermediaries and underlings. Hence often the core message was lost. This also worked in the favour of underlings who may have wanted to ensure the centre of local power remained in their hands and their interpretation of law was what was transmitted to the ordinary citizens.

Thousands of years later, when Narendra Modi reached out directly to hundreds of millions of Indians through his *Mann ki Baat*, he was channelling the same marketing genius that inspired Ashoka. Even now, Modi is working to find a way of getting his message across directly to the country's citizens. During his visit to the Facebook headquarters in September 2015, Modi was applauded by Mark Zuckerberg for his use of social media in campaigning and keeping in touch with the public. Modi talked about how leaders would sometimes need years to truly know what their citizens feel, but now with social media, he is able to establish a direct connection and receive real-time feedback. Modi is using the information highway the same way and for the same basic purpose that Ashoka used physical highways all those years ago. In doing so, these two leaders tap into a basic skill that all marketers must master: Finding the most

efficient and effective way to get their message out to the
target consumer.

Another aspect of marketing which we tend to associate
with modern technology and tools is the ability to create a
campaign or message that goes 'viral'. While the tools to
do so have certainly changed over the years, long before
Facebook, Twitter and YouTube became vehicles to carry
messages, people were using the same principles to stoke
their own movements. These are salient principles which
have stood the test of time. You need to be clear on who
you are targeting, have a message that provokes an emotional
reaction among them by playing on their hopes, aspirations
or indeed, even their fears, and then ideally have a clear call
to action that encourages people to do something (click
something, take a challenge, share the message etc.). All this
must sound like key points a young brand manager would
keep in mind while creating a new campaign today on social
media. But perhaps one of the most 'viral' campaigns in our
history that used these same principles dates back to 1857. A
campaign with very far-reaching consequences.

Everybody knows about the sepoy uprising, the cartridges
greased with cow and pig fat to incite revolt against British
officers and Mangal Pandey's role in the revolt. We have read
about and studied this revolt, which we now call the First War
of Indian Independence. The message about the new cartridges
being greased with pork and cow fat was a masterstroke. It
was built on long-simmering discontent among sepoys. These
sepoys were already resentful of their British masters and

how they were being treated. One important reason for this resentment was that these sepoys could never aspire to rise above a certain level in the ranks. The audience was perfectly chosen and the message sent out played on the fear that the British were out to destroy Indian religions. It united Hindus and Muslims in one fell swoop. We don't know today who first spread this message, but whoever it was unlocked long-held frustrations among sepoys and unleashed the first organized, large-scale revolt against the British.

The British East India Company protested that the new Enfield rifle had just been inducted. It claimed that it was aware that there would be sensitivities involved, and so the new cartridges had not actually been deployed to any sepoy contingents but merely sent in small numbers to India for field testing by British soldiers. This protest was too little, too late. This defence never reached the masses and ultimately didn't matter as their action was a late, intellectual response to something that was already unleashing an emotional firestorm. It was very much like a big brand or company issuing a boring PR statement when consumers were setting social media on fire with complaints about the product. The message of the colonial masters never really reached those whom it could have impacted—the sepoys. Instead, through word of mouth, the message of the tainted cartridges had penetrated through the ranks. The events this 'viral' message set into motion were much more important and with lasting consequences than the various challenges that go viral today on Facebook.

Later, the British Empire was formally established in India. In challenging the might of this empire, freedom fighters used some of the same principles used by branding and marketing managers, such as creating brand names that resonate with consumers and creating a strong call to action that generates action among them. A great example of this was Netaji Subhash Chandra Bose. The Azad Hind Fauj or Indian National Army was a masterstroke of branding. It unified everyone under a common banner of fighting for the nation, irrespective of which state, caste or religion one belonged to. In an age when the major political parties of the day were beginning to squabble over the rights and privileges of religious groups, Bose rose above it. The genius of his strategy was that he appealed to the Indian in all. Also, this was a time when many in the Indian middle class were content to serve their British masters, and often middle class youth were discouraged from joining the freedom struggle and instead urged to focus on their studies and careers. Bose called his group an army. Instantly, he was recruiting not for some group of rabble-rousers or troublemakers opposing the establishment, but his force *was* the establishment. He was creating a legitimate army which all Indians could join and fight in. On the other side of the fight was the army of the alien occupiers. Then came his genius of creating memorable 'selling lines'. Today, brand managers and creative directors dream of creating slogans and selling lines for their brands which would create an impact in consumer consciousness. The principles for doing so, as marketing training and textbooks tell us, is to keep the line memorable. It needs to have a clear call to action and appeal both to the heart and the mind; in other words, don't have just information, but appeal to emotions. *Chalo Dilli* was that magical slogan which galvanized millions to join the fight. Delhi was not conquered by this army. But the aftermath of its struggle, and the trial of INA officers sparked national uprisings and mutinies in the British Indian Army. This is believed to be one of the contributory factors for the ultimate demise of the British Raj.

The post-Independence period saw India trying to find its place in the world and like a new brand in a marketplace, it had to define what made it unique. In a bipolar world, with the United States and the Soviet Union carving out their spheres of influence, India chose to 'differentiate' itself by spearheading the Non-aligned Movement. It chose a path of development that was a hybrid of Soviet state planning and Western-style democracy. We were differentiated all right, though historians still argue about whether we changed fast enough as the 'marketplace' around us changed. One of the unfortunate 'brand equities' we picked up with our stuttering economy was the so-called 'Hindu rate of growth'—used to describe the narrow band of 3 to 4 per cent growth the Indian economy demonstrated, and seemed to be stuck in, for several decades after Independence. Our leaders continued to build brands around themselves and used memorable selling lines like *Garibi Hatao* to capture the popular imagination. India was fast becoming a country where votes were often sought on the brands created out of the personality cults of the leaders than any real political or economic agenda.

The Nehru–Gandhi brand had 'market leadership' for many years, with successive relaunches and brand extensions. Then this 'brand' started meeting new brands which might not have had their history and lineage, but were 'brands of the people'—embodied in statesmen like Atal Bihari Vajpayee. Then the Congress met an irresistible force in Narendra Modi's brand, which positioned itself as the very antithesis of the 'ruling' family; with his humble roots, he was a people's man, and he connected directly with his 'consumers' using branding strategies and selling lines with the genius of a veteran marketer, and then we entered the days of *Acche Din*.

Going back to Adam and his apple, the true power of stories and ideas and the impact they have on the human mind and our behaviour can be seen using the metaphor of the humble apple. The apple ties together Adam, supposedly the forefather of all humans, and us today, not philosophically or in the realms of religion, but in terms of imagery and ideas we resonate and identify with. That power of branding in recent times has been demonstrated by a company which transformed electrical gadgets and items of utility into items of desire. That company is Apple and their logo, something that would be recognizable to Adam, is a half-eaten apple on the back of every device. Apple tapped into the desire to be seen as upwardly mobile, to be set apart from others, to be seen at the cutting edge, to transform electronic gadgets which had been seen as largely utilitarian into items of desire and luxury, the same way Adam discovered desire through something that he had taken for granted and had been in front of him the whole time—the apple.

While the principles of marketing have indeed played a role in shaping our history, this book is however not one of the broad sweep of empires, fleets and marauding armies. It does not narrate to you the 'history of marketing'. Rather it intends to take the principles of marketing and show how they can be used to both better understand and influence everyday life. With a bit of understanding of how marketing really works, ordinary life and the mundane, which we take for granted, can become remarkable.

It doesn't matter if you've never studied marketing, because this is not meant to be an academic book. What I will try and do in the next few chapters is show how marketers think about influencing consumer behaviour to achieve their objectives. I will distil the key principles involved, for example, what do marketers do when facing challenges like differentiating one brand from another, making consumers more loyal, winning in new markets and so on. Then, we will explore everyday challenges and choices we all face. I have no doubt that the principles of marketing can help us make better informed and well-thought-through choices. That's what this book is all about—making connections between principles usually reserved for marketing strategy and everyday choices, because one thing unifies them: the fact that they are all about influencing human behaviour.

The application of insights to solve everyday issues is nothing new as far as India goes. Chanakya laid out the principles of governance and statecraft using his sharp insights into human behaviour in the *Arthashastra*. Manu laid out principles and thoughts about how society could be organized in the Manu *Dharma Shastra*. And then Vatsyayan and others contributed to affairs of love and passion in the body of work known as the *Kama Shastra*. This book has a scope neither as grand as statecraft nor as intimate as what you do in the privacy of your bedroom. But it covers those myriad things in between that do consume our minds and energies, those in-between the big and small things which together end up deciding how our days and years go by. This, dear reader, is an attempt to write a guide to optimize all those things which go into determining whether we are indeed creating acche din for ourselves and those around us.

I call it Brand Shastra.

2
The Shastra of Differentiation

Lessons in Becoming a Differentiated Groom

With the growing clutter of competing options in practically every industry, one of the first tasks for any modern marketer is to distinguish his or her brand from competitors. Put simply, given other options out there, why should the consumer pick your brand over another? That, in many ways, sums up the very raison d'etre of marketing. In a world where your consumers have many choices, how can you make them choose your brand by setting your market offering apart? What brand differentiation achieves is that the next time a consumer is in the market or your point of sale, you increase the chances of them identifying and remembering your offering over a potentially different choice from other competitors.

To understand how that is done, one does not need to sit in a marketing class at an IIM or a meeting room at a Procter & Gamble. One needs to just search our own history. Just over 4000 years back, to be precise, in the area that we today identify as the location of the Indus Valley Civilization. In sites throughout this area, notably in the cities of Mohenjo-daro and Harappa, archaeologists have found pottery and wares with seals. These seals show various animals and other designs. Many such square seals, and merchandise with these designs on them, have been found in sites in the distant Middle East, in what was then Mesopotamia. Many scholars believe that there was a flourishing trade between these ancient civilizations. The people of the Indus Valley used to create such wares and sell them to their trading partners in the Middle East. The trade between ancient peoples is not remarkable per se. What makes this truly remarkable is that some scholars believe this demonstrates the first known use of branding. These early manufacturers used 'brandmarks' (in the form of the seals) and other messages on their wares to set their product apart from competition. Stanley Wolpert of UCLA believes that these seals were 'probably made for merchants who used them to "brand" their wares' along with accompanying writing in a yet untranslated language.

These ancient merchants and traders were demonstrating an uncanny understanding of marketing. This understanding is taught to marketers and still practised in corporate board rooms 4000 years later.

This is nothing but the concept of using 'points of parity' and 'points of difference' in any category. It sounds dense and academic but is actually remarkably simple. Let me explain.

A point of parity is something that any brand must have in the category it is competing in to even be in the consideration set of consumers. Having a point of parity does not guarantee that a consumer will select your brand, but not having it may well rule your brand out from the nexus of options completely. For a fridge, one such obvious point of parity would be cooling, while for a laundry detergent it would be cleaning. It is essentially a feature that is common to all brands of a specific product type and necessary to deliver on the basic expectations of that product type. For example, this for our ancient marketers in the Indus Valley may have meant simply a jug which could hold water without leaking.

Once you establish points of parity, we go to the real game changers—points of difference. These features, attributes or associations which can set a brand apart from others in the category are what really get a brand noticed and picked over its competitors. These are what help a brand create presence within its product category.

For a professional marketer, there are three ways of establishing points of difference. These are:

1. By appealing to a differentiated target. In other words, appealing to consumers whom your competition may not be targeting, or who may inherently have less appeal for your competitors. A good example is Emami's Fair and Handsome cream. The fairness cream market was already pretty crowded with strong brands like Fair & Lovely but Emami managed to carve out a strong niche for itself despite being a new entrant. It created a differentiated brand by being the first to target a fairness cream at men, interestingly based on the insight that many men were using their wives' fairness creams.

2. By offering a benefit or feature that is different or better than what other competitors do. Sometimes, these points of differentiation are simply delivering better performance on the points of parity. An example would be a laundry detergent claiming it cleans better or faster than its market counterpart. However, sometimes the most powerful differentiators are when a brand offers

benefits which have not been offered before in the category, or when it creates a very different way for the consumer to experience old benefits. Look at the smartphone category. Its consumers had long evolved from using phones only for making calls. They were now taking for granted that they could use them to send email, access the Internet and perform many of the rudimentary tasks of a computer. Then came the iPhone. It really set itself apart over the years, not just with its design and interface, but by bringing the entire ecosystem of 'Apps' with it. Over time, other manufacturers have arguably caught up with Apple on design and interface, but the ecosystem of Apps continues to remain a point of differentiation for many consumers. Going back to the Indus Valley Civilization, manufacturers may have all made jugs equally suited for carrying or serving water, but what those early marketers sought to do was perhaps to use distinctive designs to transform a humble jug into a decorative object that a Mesopotamian housewife would have been proud to display. For those ancient marketers, like Apple, design and aesthetic were the key points of difference.

3. Breaking the clutter, which entails communicating with a consumer in a disruptive way, is sometimes a great way to get into a consumer's mind and set your brand apart. In others words, creating points of difference based on occupying a disproportionate share of the consumers'

mind through significantly heavier media or in-store presence than competitors, or a provocative message that gets a brand noticed and talked about. A recent example would be housing.com's high-impact Look Up campaign. Reportedly up to Rs 120 crore was spent on this campaign which involved print, billboards and digital channels. Housing.com plastered its logo and the line '#lookup' in several cities across India. It was hard to miss it. Everyone was talking about it. In press reports of the time, the housing.com marketing team claimed an increase in traffic of 500 per cent. It clearly broke the clutter and set itself apart from other brands in the space, not because of its message per se, but because of the sheer omnipresence that made it hard to miss. But it was also a cautionary tale. It showed that depending on just the 'how' without having a clearly defined 'what' can be counterproductive. There was a lot of criticism about this campaign being a waste of investors' money. Some said that it did not actually translate into any incremental revenue. Critics panned the effort saying that not much was conveyed in the housing.com ads other than the two vague words, 'look up'.

• • •

But what is the relevance of all this talk on differentiation in our everyday life? How will the understanding of these concepts help us find better solutions to everyday problems?

We choose between alternative options all the time, and sometimes this also applies to people, in addition to things. And indeed, pitching ourselves for being chosen over others is a practice that we are also quite used to. Anyone who has applied for a job or tried to woo someone in love knows this. We are always striving to stand out from other competing 'brands' to achieve what we want. This is something that is inherently part of our personal and professional lives.

I'm sure you have applied for a job where you wondered if your résumé had enough in it to set you apart, or if you are as old as me, spent a lot of time thinking about which school you'd want to send your child to. That is a decision my wife and I recently grappled with. We went through the same thought process that consumers go through when choosing a brand off the shelf. We researched the schools. We asked other parents who had sent their kids there and went to check them out ourselves before making a decision. How a school tries to stand out was also similar to how most consumer brands try to differentiate themselves, because when you're trying to compete in a cluttered choice set, whether you're a detergent brand on a shelf, a school trying to attract applicants, or a job seeker pursuing a dream job, you need to try and set yourself apart while ensuring you don't miss on the 'minimum requirements'. There were some obvious points of parity (basic facilities, classrooms, transport arrangements) but what was interesting was the points of differences different schools focused on (small class size and therefore more individual attention for some, top-of-the-line facilities for another, reputation through alumni or word of mouth for others).

That's because wherever there is a choice to be made between options, the human psyche makes us evaluate the choices by considering not just the rational risks and returns but also the emotions associated with each choice. We immediately look at what is similar and common between choices. Then we focus on what makes each choice stand apart. That 'apartness' is what makes a choice get noticed, and the relevance or attractiveness of that difference is what gets something to be preferred. The thinking of how marketers seek to differentiate brands can help us make better choices in terms of decoding how choices are presented to us. By the same principle, we can make ourselves a more attractive choice for others.

We see such choices and attempts to set choices apart being made all around us—not just in industries and fields which we relate brand management with but also life. Sometimes, it is based on genuine, well-considered differentiation, and sometimes, it is just trying to project difference where no meaningful difference may really exist. A classic example that comes to mind is that of the age-old Bollywood director. He makes the most formulaic masala film with melodrama and item numbers, and then speaks in an interview about how his latest offering is different (*'yeh film kuch hatke hai!'*).

On a larger canvas, the 2014 Indian elections saw a classic use of parties differentiating their prime ministerial candidates based on what was supposedly unique to them. So Modi's humble origins (and the coloured tales of him selling tea on railway platforms) was milked for all it was worth. He was projected as the 'common man's' candidate. And that kind of branding genius, usually associated with consumer marketing, got extended to other properties like *Chai pe Charcha*. When some Congress spokespersons tried to belittle this 'status', it backfired. That was the brilliance of this campaign. It not only played on the 'rags to riches' story that resonated emotionally with many voters, but played on the dissatisfaction with the current regime by portraying Modi as the polar opposite of the ruling party candidate. The opposition leader's comments just further elevated the projection of Modi as a humble 'everyman' versus the supposedly 'dynastic' and 'privileged' Congress candidate.

You can see this differentiation sometimes closer to home in everyday choices we make about our lives. I remember back at IIM, the usual rush to brush up résumés before placement. People had so much anxiety on meeting the criteria that each particular company was 'looking for'. Putting in extra-curricular activities to project themselves apart, ironically, started becoming the norm.

So whether it is a Bollywood director or a young jobseeker, the same psychology is at work. We are all trying to answer one common question. How do I set myself apart to increase chances of being selected or preferred?

• • •

To help illustrate the importance of differentiation further with another real-life example, let's dig deeper into a massive Indian marketplace, where, every single year, many millions of choices and preferences are exercised. Like in all cases, some options are chosen over others and these options often compete aggressively for their 'consumers'. In this race, each is trying to pitch themselves as the most attractive choice.

While this may apply to any marketplace, I am specifically talking about the great Indian marriage bazaar.

By most accounts, the 'market' for marriages in India is huge. Trade magazines claim that the total expense on weddings in India could up be upwards of Rs 1,00,000 crore a year. This figure is not surprising given that the average number of weddings per day is pegged at around 25,000.

That's a lot of weddings! And behind each of those weddings is a fundamental choice being made. This choice is more important and with longer lasting implications than the simple choice of a smartphone or laundry detergent. Each person getting married has to choose between options for suitable partners, especially if one goes through the traditional route of having options being presented by parents, family, nosy neighbours, marriage bureaus or matrimonial ads. So how do the principles of points of parity and points of difference apply to this 'market' and what more can we learn from them in this application?

I studied the matrimonial ads for grooms in one particular Sunday *Times of India* (Mumbai edition). There were 130 ads on that Sunday, yet immediately some things were evident.

As would be intuitive, the Indian marriage market operates on a pretty basic starting point of targeting by communities. So the primary way in which ads were 'targeted' were by caste or community, perhaps an unfortunate comment on how we still divide ourselves along these lines. So if you're Bengali and insist on a Bengali groom for yourself or your daughter, there's a convenient column for that. Also, if you are agnostic to the caste or community, there are categories called 'caste no bar' and 'cosmopolitan'. And if you happen to fit into a very specific target audience, there is a separate group for 'second marriages'. So far, so good. This is because this is still the basis on which a number of choices are made in terms of finding the right groom.

Second, the principle of differentiating the matrimonial ad by showing up in a disruptive way (differentiating based on the 'how') in the consumer's mind is important. Seven ads were highlighted in separate boxes and in larger fonts—in marketing terms, paying to have a higher 'share of voice' and a matrimonial ad equivalent to the housing.com billboard blitz.

However, what is truly interesting is when we look at the differentiation based on the 'what'. What attributes are potential grooms and their families advertising and what does this tell us about the points of parity and difference in this market?

Three clear points of parity emerge, mentioned in at least 50 per cent of the ads. The market dynamics are such that not mentioning these would mean a very low response and that these constitute the 'minimum category' information. It is similar to the 'need to deliver on cleaning for laundry detergent' example we talked about earlier. In descending order, these are:

Height: 96 per cent of ads
Educational qualifications: 65 per cent of ads
Job status: 59 per cent of ads

Now let's assume you are 'in the market' for yourself or for your daughter and are looking for a suitable groom. Now that you're facing a number of options of tall, educated and employed grooms, how do you choose between them? What makes any of them stand out?

Clearly, one principle is employed which any marketer will resonate with, which is amplifying the points of parity (not just educated, but with a degree from IIT/IIM, not just with a good job but with a multinational firm, etc.). At least 30 per cent of ads mentioned an elaboration of these points of parity. But what was fascinating is how else people tried to differentiate, and there was no one clear approach on this front. Here was the additional information supplied, in an attempt to differentiate the grooms:

Attribute	Per Cent of Ads	Additional Comments
Income	28	Refers to ads with a specific number mentioned when it comes to salary or income.
Looks	28	Most common being 'handsome' though one did mention 'strong build', presumably in case you want a bodyguard in addition to a groom.
Living abroad	19	Explicit mention of being NRIs/settled abroad—vast majority being in the United States.
Family background	17	Usually talk about the father's job or position, or indeed, a flourishing family business where applicable.
Fair complexion	15	Certainly will gladden the hearts of the marketers of fairness creams that a full 15 per cent of grooms and their families felt that mentioning a fair complexion would set them apart.

One observation is certain: There is no one obvious differentiator. As with brands in any other category, you play to your strengths. If you have a fancy degree, you flaunt it; if you earn a high salary, you brag about it; and indeed, if you think you are fair, you talk about it. While these may sound like understandable criteria based on which differentiation would occur, here are a few remarks that may help the prospective groom and his family successfully set themselves apart, building off some of the basics of marketing.

The first observation is that many of these advertisers were deficient as they did not venture beyond the points of parity. A full 22 per cent of the ads mentioned at most the points of parity, and a full 50 per cent of these did not even cover all three points of parity mentioned above. That's almost a quarter of the ads showing up with the same appeal as, say, a box of detergent on a shelf with the claim 'I clean clothes'. In the competitive set of the sort we see in this one-day's sample of ads, these 22 per cent of ads have very little chance of being noticed because they are not offering any additional information other than what are almost category 'hygiene factors', i.e. no points of difference that may help set them apart. A marketer looking at this information will conclude that being tall and having a degree is not enough. You need to really think about what sets you apart and highlight that.

Marketing is about getting the consumer to choose you. In other words, marketers need to have a huge degree of humility. You are acknowledging that the consumer is boss and that while you are putting your best foot forward and presenting your case, you are doing so with an attempt to best understand the consumer and meet his or her needs. You cannot badger or pressure the consumer to choose you. That sounds pretty basic and all of us would empathize with the sentiment given that the same principle holds when we are interacting with anyone. Something you don't need to go to business school or work in marketing to figure out, right? However, 19 per cent of the ads devoted at least as much space to saying what they expected the prospective bride to be, instead of talking about what their 'brand' offered. That's like a brand devoting half of its TV advertising time talking about what kind of consumer 'deserves' to use their brand, instead of why the brand is worthy of the consumer. If you saw such an ad, you would no doubt be pissed off. Then imagine the chances of the following ad in generating appeal among prospective takers: 'Very fair wrkg in US boy seeks v.fair, beautiful, prof. qualified girl from affluent family'.

Okay, so you want everything one could want in a girl (beautiful, rich, qualified), and what exactly does your son bring to the party other than copious usage of Fair and Handsome and a green card?

Ads such as these, which spent most of their word count focused on making demands on the prospective bride were also the ones that much more than average, focused only on points of parity. Thirty-six per cent of these ads mentioned at most the points of parity and no points of difference, and a full 41 per cent of all ads that made no mention of one of the possible points of difference identified above were those which made demands on the girls instead of focusing on what the groom brought to the table. In other words, the odds are really stacked against some of these ads as they focus not on what sets their 'brand' apart but on who they want their consumer to be.

This analysis also bears out the reality of the marketing landscape, where the top three or four brands will often have upwards of 50 per cent market share while there will be a long tail of wannabes. In this small sample of the Indian matrimonial market, it is pretty clear what that tail is.

Finally, it is not enough to just have things that are unique to you, but to also have those points of difference be meaningful to your consumer. A brand of detergent may indeed have pink polka dot packaging, and may also be the only brand in the whole market that has it, but is unlikely to garner much sales if that means nothing to prospective consumers. So, what do we know about what the Indian consumer—in this case, prospective brides and their families—want from a groom? To understand that, let's dip into surveys done by shaadi.com, whose business is to find the best match possible for prospective brides and grooms:

The reassuring part for those who used some of the points of difference in the ads discussed above is that some of those things *do* seem to matter. Ninety-four per cent of women in these surveys prefer a partner who earns more than them; 69 per cent prefer a partner with a job in the private sector or multinationals and 69 per cent prefer a husband who is more

educated than them. So those talking about salaries, MNC
jobs and degrees from top-notch schools are indeed playing
to the right points of difference by elaborating on the specifics
of their education or employment in an attempt to stand out.

Bad news for the fairness cream users, though. Only
25 per cent of women in these surveys said their partner's
complexion mattered. For 65 per cent of respondents, it
did not matter if the prospective groom was fair. So the
15 per cent of ads in the sample that talked about fair
complexion were perhaps wasting money and space.

When it comes to demands on the women, the vast
majority talked about wanting 'beautiful' girls or those with
'values'. What the shaadi.com surveys point out is that more
than being treated as a beautiful object to decorate the home,
Indian women want their individuality to be valued. Close
to 50 per cent consider being treated with respect as a major
criterion in choosing a partner, and it's a safe bet that the ads
that make demands of the girl on purely physical attributes
will likely not find many takers among these women.

Finally, there is something that none of these ads even
touch on, yet which is perhaps emerging as an important
factor. A full 51.2 per cent of women in these surveys want a
partner who can help with household chores and 39.5 per cent
want a husband who can cook. In other words, pick up your
cookbook and drop the fairness cream tube and you could be
on your way to being a more differentiated groom.

• • •

THE THREE MANTRAS OF THE SHASTRA OF DIFFERENTIATION

- What's your point? Be aware of and sufficiently expansive on the points of parity but understand and use your points of difference as well—this is what will set you apart.
- Being noticed does not just mean being the loudest voice around. Don't be different for the sake of standing out, but do it when you're offering something meaningful.
- Beware of the 'fairness cream trap'. Don't offer something just because others are doing it. Do your homework on whether that quality is really desirable among your 'consumers'.

3

The Shastra of Trial and Preference

Understanding Your Moments of Truth at Work

It is an old marketing adage that perception is reality. What that means is, when consumers make a choice, whether to buy a shampoo or a particular brand of car, only a small part of that decision-making process is driven by rational facts or scientifically-tested data on performance. In fact, many of those decisions are taken based on perceptions formed through a number of factors—advertising, past experience, what they have heard from others, etc. One of the first things a young marketer has to confront is this reality of *how* consumer decisions in the real world of marketing are made, and then adapt to it accordingly.

Many bright MBAs, armed with degrees in engineering and business theories and models (who excel at finding rational, fact-based answers to problems), struggle when faced with this ambiguous and fickle nature of real-world consumer decision-making. One can even say that the situation could be summed up by introducing these MBAs to Shakespeare who said, 'Beauty is in the eye of the beholder.' They could learn a lot by understanding this simple statement. Over time, marketers have learned not to elaborate on how much more beautiful their brand is, based on how they would like consumers to see it. Instead, they are focusing on understanding the eye of the beholder and how they perceive beauty.

Over the years, marketers have come to think of this process through what are called 'moments of truth'. Procter & Gamble kicked off the conversation on this coinage by introducing a concept called the 'first moment of truth', which is when the consumer first comes face to face with your brand on the store shelf. At this point, the consumer makes a choice—whether to pick up your brand or a competitor's. Google took this forward (or a step back, in this case) by introducing the concept of 'zero moment of truth'. So what are these moments of truth and how do marketers plan using them?

The zero moment of truth (ZMOT) is when consumers are exposed to information (or find it, if they seek it out) about a potential purchase. This can be through exposure to advertising, and even just a decade ago, brand advertising on television or radio would have been the primary source of this. Increasingly, consumers are actively seeking out information online to find out more about brands and products. This due diligence is helping to shape their choice of which brand they will buy even before they walk into a store. Google pioneered the thinking about the zero moment of truth and in extensive studies carried out in the United States in 2011, Google research showed some pretty fascinating findings. As expected, consumers looked at more sources to decide on a purchase for categories which had more risk/investment than those which had lower investment or risk, but what was fascinating is that in some categories, up to 97 per cent of the final purchase decision was influenced at the zero moment of truth. In other words, an electronics manufacturer could spend countless hours finessing the product features and having the spiffiest showrooms, but would start with a distinct disadvantage versus its competitors if the consumer searched online and decided that this brand was not for them based on information or reviews they found online. Also fascinating was the sheer number of sources consulted in some high-involvement categories, indicating that in today's marketplace, there is no one silver bullet to create consumer demand. Here is a sampling of data from the survey that reveals how shoppers are influenced at the ZMOT, across some pretty diverse categories as reproduced in the well-known marketing blog 'Actionable Marketing Guide' run by marketing guru and author Heidi Cohen:[1]

Category	Number of Sources Used by Typical Shopper	Per Cent Shoppers Influenced by ZMOT
Automotive	18.2	97
Consumer Electronics	14.8	92
Health, Personal, Beauty Care	7	63
Quick Service Restaurants	5.8	72

The first moment of truth (FMOT), introduced by Procter & Gamble, described the real moment of truth for a brand as when its consumer sees it on a shelf, next to its competitors, and has to decide which brand to pick up. This was based on the insight that even if you created awareness and strong demand beforehand, often consumer choice was swung while in-store, due to a number of factors—packaging, claims, displays in stores, pricing and so on. The number widely quoted at the time was that 70 per cent of purchase decisions are made in-store. This is a bit of an oversimplification and perhaps contradicts the data on ZMOT quoted above. However, the impact of what happens at the point of purchase is undeniable. In a very comprehensive study spanning twenty-four markets and 14,000 shoppers, OgilvyAction showed that indeed, brand switches do happen in stores though the percentage differs by category and kind of store.[2]

For small *kirana* stores of the kind we see in India, many consumers decide the brand they want before they go shopping or based on past habits and perceptions. This is because unlike a supermarket, the store environment does not allow the kind of browsing and comparison required for brand switching. However, what this study also showed is that beyond brand choice, what happens in-store can determine whether a consumer buys a particular category at all. Twenty per cent of shoppers impulsively bought a category they had no intention of buying based on what they saw in-store. Ten per cent did not buy a category that was on their list, because it was too hard to find or did not stand out.

Now as the shopping landscape has changed, what happens in front of a store shelf happens on a tablet or smartphone screen as well, as consumers compare deals and prices on e-commerce sites. But the rules of the game stay the same: make a great first impression (claims, packs, value, deals) or be left out of the shopping basket.

The 'second moment of truth' (SMOT) was another phrase popularized by Procter & Gamble. It described what happens when the consumer actually uses the product or service. Great messaging and in-store appearance can get you a trial, but the only way a consumer will come back for a second helping is if the actual usage experience was satisfactory. Part of the SMOT is the product or service itself, but a large part of it is also perceived value. In other words, was the experience seen as 'worth it', especially enough to deserve another visit? To use an analogy from a different industry, you may find a new restaurant on the Internet or see its advertising in the local paper; you may have a very pleasant FMOT when you see the decor and the menu. However, a poor SMOT, whether it is sloppy service or food that is not up to expectations, will probably ensure you don't go back.

The final moment of truth is called the 'third moment of truth'. This is when a satisfied consumer actually starts becoming an advocate for the brand and starts sharing goodwill about the brand. In the old days, this was called word of mouth, because that's literally how this information was spread. With technology and the explosion of social media, word of mouth has transformed in terms of speed of reaction and also reach. Today, with 140 characters and a press of the 'enter' button, a brand can gain thousands of new fans or have its promises and reputation put into question. Data from the market research firm, Nielsen in the United States showed that 92 per cent of consumers would believe recommendations from family or friends over any advertising. Marketers are also beginning to realize this with data from the American Marketing Association showing that 64 per cent of marketers believe that word of mouth is the most effective form of marketing. That is why so many companies are investing in resources and capabilities to engage effectively with consumers online.[3]

So, being a successful marketer and building a brand that really stands both the test of time and consumer scrutiny means focusing on things beyond just creating great advertising or having a great product. It means taking a holistic view of all these four moments of truth and delighting consumers better than competition at each of these intervals.

• • •

These concepts of consumer marketing have a far broader applicability in our world. We often have to make choices where we have to consider multiple factors, or get information about our choices in multiple 'moments of truth' or stages, with added information impacting how we feel about that choice. To carry forward the matrimonial ad analogy of the previous chapter, let's say the parents of a girl see an ad that gets them interested. That prospective groom would have entered their consideration set, but has so far only passed the zero moment of truth. The first moment of truth comes when the boy and girl, perhaps with families in tow, come face to face. If the boy comes across as a bore, or has aspects to his personality that at first glance don't really hit it off with the girl and her family, or indeed if the reality of meeting a person in flesh and blood isn't everything that interesting matrimonial ad seemed to promise, then our groom has failed the first moment of truth. The second moment of truth comes when, if things progress, typically the girl and boy get to spend more time together and get to know each other better. As they know each other more, deeper aspects of the person, including his values, his views on various matters, how he relates to people etc. come out into the open, and again the girl and her family have an opportunity to assess whether they are making the right choice or not. The third moment of truth comes because, in most cases, the parents and the girl would not want to make such a big commitment without checking references. They would usually ask around among friends and relatives, or even get a proper background check done. If any major issues crop up here, things could get derailed. So, writing that perfect matrimonial ad may get you a foot in the door, but there's still many a slip between the cup and the lip— that first meeting and actually going off on a honeymoon with the bride of your dreams.

In my personal life, I see this play out as well all the time. Reading is something I'm passionate about, and I get most of my reading done on the Kindle. I may hear of a new book in the media, or indeed get a title recommended by Amazon or friends. The FMOT comes when I actually visit that book's Amazon page, and see the cover and read the blurb. In the digital age, the first and third moments of truth often coincide, because seeking recommendations is not a sequential task. I can read the reviews right there on the book's webpage and start forming an opinion of whether I'd be interested in reading the book or not. When I download and read it, the second moment of truth kicks in, and if I have a positive experience, that writer gains a loyal reader, as I'll often actively seek out other work by him or her. Word of mouth could also be generated. I may recommend this writer or book to friends and family. On the other hand, a negative experience at the second moment of truth would mean that even if the writer writes a book in the future that I might well enjoy, I will perhaps be more circumspect about choosing it.

Both examples bring out how the thinking around moments of truth is a powerful way to break down our decision-making process when we're choosing anything. This could apply to a life partner, a book or indeed even choosing our country's leaders.

In the 2014 Lok Sabha elections, all key political parties had spent hundreds of crores in building up their leaders and projecting them as the best prime ministerial candidate. One incident comes to mind, when a potential candidate failed the first moment of truth. People had perceptions and ideas about Rahul Gandhi, the scion of India's first political family and leader of the Congress party. These were both positive and negative perceptions based on political affiliation but people still did not know much about this young leader. Till then, he had never before appeared in a one-on-one interview. This changed when he stepped into the studio to chat with Arnab Goswami in January 2014. In many ways, it was his first moment of truth with the Indian electorate. The general consensus was that he did not come off as positively as he, and his party, would have liked. First off, it was his body language. Don't take my word for it. Here is what the *New York Times* said about it: 'Mr Gandhi fumbled, stared with a blank expression and a tilted head and looked wounded at times.' From a marketer's standpoint, what was also apparent was that he did not have any real point of difference to offer. He focused his conversation on three areas—women's empowerment, youth involvement and the Right to Information (RTI) Act. All of these are relevant issues, but none, individually or collectively, showed him as offering a very differentiated or particularly desirable viewpoint versus his competitor, Narendra Modi. Finally, to that end, he came across as being a reluctant leader, the opposite of someone looking to take on the competition and offer a confident, bold vision of what he would offer as a leader. In the course of the interview, Arnab mentioned Narendra Modi by name twenty-eight times and asked pointed questions about whether Rahul saw himself as being projected as the Congress prime ministerial candidate in direct opposition to Modi. Rahul Gandhi's replies seemed vague or evasive. He seemed not to want to mention Modi at all, preferring to say 'the BJP's prime ministerial candidate'. Compared to Modi, who was clearly projected as the candidate for prime minister, and offering a promise of strong, clear leadership, Rahul waffled when it came to being named the Congress's prime ministerial candidate, even though it was painfully obvious to anyone that he would be the candidate they would project as the prime minister if the Congress won. This particular exchange is worth reproducing to contrast the directness and pointedness of Arnab's question and the long-winded response:[4]

ARNAB: See Rahul we can go up and down on this question. The fact of the matter is this, who else will they choose, and who else will Congress MPs choose if not Rahul Gandhi?

RAHUL: That is up to them right, but what one has to do, and this is central to what I keep saying, is that democracy is about respect of processes. Democracy is about non-arbitrary decisions. Democracy is about spreading decisions; it is not about destroying processes. There is a process in the constitution and that process says, and it is clearly written in the constitution, and it says members of parliament are to be elected by the population and members of parliament are to elect the prime minister. All I am doing is respecting that process.

The third moment of truth came in as this interview began trending on Twitter and sound bites were being shared on Facebook. Perhaps in part this shaped the way the Indian electorate voted for who they would want to lead them. In May 2014, the Narendra Modi-led BJP won a landslide victory and decimated the Congress.

• • •

Now let's take this learning and apply it to yet another everyday phenomenon so many of us deal with. Here too, it seems like perception counts for more than what we assume to be 'reality'.

I'm talking about appraisals at work.

If you work in an office, or have a friend or family member who does, then you will know the angst and anxiety which accompanies the ritual of the annual appraisal. Rare is the employee who feels that he or she has been fairly assessed and those with poor ratings no doubt feel that their work has not been adequately recognized. Sometimes even those with better ratings often question why their rating or subsequent increment or promotion was not faster or higher. Part of this is human psychology at work.

We are always inherently uncomfortable about giving up control of our destiny to others. The appraisal system means that our annual rating, and the important and material impact of that in terms of salary or career progress, depends on someone else's judgement or perception of us and our performance.

Yes, several organizations try and make the appraisal system more interactive. There are systems where the employee inputs his/her view in the appraisal form. Some companies also encourage frequent feedback, so that the employee does not just get one number at the end of the year. Unfortunately, the angst about the perceived fairness, or rather lack of it, of most appraisal systems still continues to be widespread.

The market research firm Gallup has done several studies on employee perceptions of performance appraisal systems in the Indian context. The report concluded that, 'Our analysis of the data shows that companies in India struggle because many employees doubt whether a performance management system can actually identify superior performance. They also question whether these systems effectively reward good performance. These emotional responses affect employees' perceptions of how robust the system is and whether it can distribute rewards fairly and effectively.'[5]

In 2010, Gallup asked employees in several different industries across India for their opinions on various aspects of how their performance is assessed. Gallup found that Indian employees, especially those with three to ten years of experience within an organization, strongly feel that most performance appraisal systems are not capable of distinguishing superior performance. Unfortunately for managers and executives, there is a strong relationship between this perception and an employee's level of engagement in his or her workplace. More than half of the employees who disagreed with the statement, 'The performance appraisal system at my company clearly distinguishes superior performance' were what Gallup defined as 'actively disengaged'. The terminology of 'actively disengaged', as Gallup defines it, is worth calling out. These employees ' . . . aren't just unhappy at work, they are busy acting out their unhappiness. Every day, these workers undermine what their engaged coworkers accomplish.'

Clearly the perception of an unfair appraisal system leads to more than half the employees being in such a lacklustre state. Hence, the issue is not just one of employee angst but something that can actually materially derail any business or organization. For most employees, this perception of 'unfairness' comes from the belief that their 'work' is not being acknowledged. As a CEO, I have had to do many of these appraisals. I've so often encountered people who rattle off their sales figures and target accomplishments and then wonder why their rating was not better. You can't really blame them. Our educational system, by and large, has been one where we reduce an individual's worth and accomplishment level to a single number or rank in an exam. Our educational system has historically been made up of a series of single 'moments of truth'—board exams, entrance examinations (whether IIT, medical or CAT and other exams) and so on. So it's natural that many people young in their careers take the same approach in the workplace, assuming a number (sales, costs, or whatever it is they are measured on) is the only variable that will determine their assessment.

The trap they are falling into is focusing on only one of the moments of truth (the second moment, in this case) and ignoring the rest. Real-life workplaces (and real life of course) are more complex than our examination systems. Just as a marketer needs to consider all moments of truth, an employee also needs to understand and leverage all stages to increase the chances of their true contribution and potential being recognized, or at least, to feel more at peace with how they have been assessed.

In an office context, the zero moment of truth is what your manager learns about you and your profile from past appraisals or records. Instead of focusing on only short-term results and numbers, you would do well to step back and look at the track record you're building (or in branding terms, the 'equity' you have been building).

If you have a track record of patchy performance, but have a good year, don't assume a great rating is your prerogative. If anything, your boss may be wondering if these results are a flash in the pan—this may just be a one-off thing. The best thing to do in such a case is to confront it, and talk to your manager about past issues, acknowledge any lapses or set the context, and commit to improving. That way, your manager sees your results as the outcome of a concerted effort to improve, instead of thinking that 'you got lucky'. Just making that effort to confront any past identified issues or weaknesses and declare to work on them in itself will show a high level of maturity and self-awareness that will serve you well.

By doing this, you are intervening on how your manager takes the zero moment of truth instead of leaving him or her to draw their own conclusions. Even if your track record is very good and there are only positives in past assessments, build off those positives. Talk about how you'd like to stretch more and develop yourself, perhaps by taking on more challenging work. You then build off the past bank of positive equity instead of just relying on this year's results.

The first moment of truth is how you show up when you interact with your managers and peers. Sometimes people focus only on the 'results'—in communicating with others, they focus on just 'getting the point across'. In doing so they make the assumption that simply because they have the 'right answer', they should be fine. Again this is a legacy of an educational system which oversimplifies definitions of success and where marks are given for getting the 'one right answer' and solving a problem the 'right way'. This system does not prepare students for the ambiguity and many potential choices to solve real-life issues in the workplace. The reality of human psychology is very different. Just as consumers could be put off a brand because of packaging or design, even if the product inside is the best in the world, your managers and peers react to much more than your 'content' when it comes to forming impressions.

Professor Albert Mehrabian of UCLA is a global expert on non-verbal cues in communication and his research in the matter has thrown up some truly mind-opening results. His work focuses on understanding what an audience reacts to most when listening to a speaker. Here are his findings on what determines the audience's takeaway from what a speaker is saying.[6]

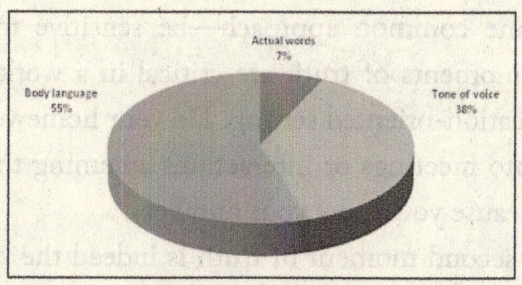

Next time you're in that presentation with your bosses, remember those numbers. How you say things and come across may count for much more than what you say. You may know your stuff, but if you come across as diffident when the job calls for strong leadership, or arrogant when it calls for subtle navigation, then you could well be setting yourself up for failure. It may seem unfair, but we all form opinions of people based on how they present themselves. It is important not just to behave in one particular 'right' way but to understand what the job at hand requires, which may change from task to task. The right approach is to show up in a way that reinforces your boss's faith in your ability to deliver.

If your current project requires decisive action, don't show up and present ten options and waffle about the intellectual challenges of coming up with all of them. Propose one point of view that is clearly backed up by sound reasoning. If there is a tough decision to be taken and there are conflicting points of view, don't show up as arguing with colleagues and become part of the problem. Instead, try and moderate the discussion and show maturity while leading the resolution. There is no one right answer, but there is one common approach—be sensitive to the fact that first moments of truth are critical in a workplace and communication-oriented setting. Do your homework before rushing into meetings or interactions assuming that all will be well because you know your numbers.

The second moment of truth is indeed the time when actual results are delivered. In most organizational contexts, delivery of results is honestly a point of parity. Unless you've blown past your objectives, just hitting targets will by itself not give you a great rating or appraisal because most organizations take meeting targets as 'meeting expectations'. If you've met or modestly exceeded your numbers, don't sit back and think that all you want by way of ratings or increments are automatically going to be heading your way. That's when you need to think of what the zero and first moments of truth are setting you up for, since assessments and perceptions formed on those will often differentiate you from employees with similar short-term results.

The third moment of truth is of course what your 'consumers' at the workplace, your peers and those who report to you, say about you. That's why most organizations have some form of feedback process to get evaluations about you from those who work with you. The feedback process is designed to check not just what the results were that you delivered, but how you delivered them, and importantly, how you worked with other people in the organization around you. So in many organizations, people with results that otherwise appear good are assessed poorly because of 'how' they were achieved. If they were not collaborative, or undermined other team members, or did not give others credit or delivered the numbers at the cost of making their employees demotivated, even good-looking numbers will not lead to a great assessment. Typically in most organizations, this is also an important way in which managers assess an employee's potential. That is, can that employee not just deliver in the here and now, but also be a part of the organization at more senior levels with increased levels of responsibility? There is no real way to 'game' this system. You just have to treat all your stakeholders fairly and with respect and realize that while the results matter, how you deliver them is equally important. What people say about you and the impact you've had on them while delivering those numbers counts for a lot.

Marketers use the moments of truth to drive trial and preference for their brands. Similarly I hope this chapter equips you with some of that same thinking to drive positive perceptions not just in your workplace but in other contexts in life as well. Your success will depend on perceptions others are forming of you and knowing and using your own moments of truth is critical to achieving that.

Just as driving trial is important, in the same way (or even more) building a sustainable business is also crucial. This is the challenge of converting those who have simply tried the brand into loyal users. These users stick with the brand over the long-term. Let's now move on to how marketers tackle this challenge of building loyalty.

● ● ●

THE THREE MANTRAS OF THE SHASTRA OF TRIAL AND PREFERENCE

- The cliché is true that you don't get a second chance to make a first impression, but in making any choice or preference, your own 'consumers' look for more than one impression. Understand what those impressions or moments of truth are and be conscious of how you show up at each.

- Don't just focus on the *what*, but on the *how* as well. In real life, whether in the workplace or in relationships, you don't always win by having one 'right' answer but by also how you manage situations and people in arriving at solutions.

- Don't dismiss gossip and be sensitive to who or what you gossip about. What seems idle gossip can be forming a third moment of truth in people's minds.

4

The Shastra of Building Loyalty

Lessons in Frequent Flyer Parenting

YOU SAID I WOULD BE UPGRADED IF I DID MY HOMEWORK EVERY DAY. WHERE ARE MY GOLD CLASS BENEFITS?

Once a marketer has managed to convince a consumer to try his or her brand based on points of difference and by showing up appropriately at the moments of truth . . . mission accomplished, right?

Wrong.

Any professional marketer will know that getting a consumer to try their brand once is just the beginning. The much harder task is to get a consumer to stick with the brand over the long-term. Whether it is a shampoo, a hotel or an airline, the true test of getting a consumer hooked to your brand is not just getting them to try it once, but to make them loyal to it. In marketing lingo, the vast majority of businesses and brands have what are called 'leaky buckets'. You keep getting consumers into the fold, but unless you make efforts to keep those consumers loyal, you also keep losing consumers. That's why loyalty programmes are such a rage, and almost all of us are greeted with various cards, schemes and loyalty rewards when we shop. There's a very good reason for that—loyal consumers give much more value, especially over the long-term.

A study by Bain Consulting in 2008 on the financial services sector showed that loyal customers (what they called 'promoters') yield almost three-and-a-half times the lifetime profits of a 'passive' customer.[1] A passive customer is someone who does not repeat purchases with the same frequency. But this is not just because a more loyal consumer will buy your brand or services more often. As the study showed, the biggest difference comes from the fact that a loyal consumer will spread positive word of mouth, encouraging others to follow suit. I discussed the power of the third moment of truth in the previous chapter. That is sometimes the true power of brand loyalty. You not only get loyal consumers to buy into your brand repeatedly, but their endorsement and positive word of mouth gets many more new consumers into the fold.

While such programmes differ in how they are executed across industries, there are some common themes. Strange as it may seem, to understand the underlying insights into human behaviour that underpin most such loyalty programmes, we do not need to attend a class at a business school or read up a marketing textbook. Instead, we owe most of those insights to a failed novelist, some small animals and a box.

B.F. Skinner (1904–90) was a scientist who, other than the few years when he dabbled unsuccessfully at writing, devoted most of his working years to understanding human behaviour (especially what determined our response to stimuli). He did this through a series of experiments involving animals placed in a box, which came to be known as the Skinner Box, named after him. Skinner created this model while he was a graduate student at Harvard in 1930, and this chamber or box allowed him and researchers to study behaviour conditioning among small animals placed in a box (now you also know where the phrase 'lab rat' comes from!) by teaching a subject animal to perform certain actions like pressing a lever in response to specific stimuli, such as a light or sound signal. When the subject correctly performs the behaviour, the chamber mechanism delivers food or another reward. In some cases, the mechanism delivers a punishment for incorrect or missing responses.

Skinner noticed that when a particular behaviour was rewarded, the chances of it being repeated increased exponentially. He called this positive reinforcement. Conversely, when a certain kind of behaviour met with negative or undesirable consequences, it decreased. Put simply, getting someone to do more of something required positive reinforcement, while getting something undesirable to stop required punishment.

This is the first principle on which almost all loyalty programmes run. Consumers are given positive reinforcement to encourage them to fly an airline more often, shop at a store more often, or stay at a hotel more often. That reinforcement takes different forms, from discounts to lounge access to upgrades. However, fundamentally, every time you smile when you are offered an upgrade by your favourite airline, you have a lot in common with a rat from fifty years ago who pressed a lever in a corner of a small box and was delighted to get a drop of sugar solution. This basic understanding of human behaviour in fact predates Skinner. Ancient marketers were using this insight long before Skinner put his rats in his box. There is evidence that in ancient Turkey, merchants were giving coupons to their customers such that every fifth purchase would be free.

The second principle of loyalty programmes again goes back well beyond current marketing theory. It simply has to do with the basic human insight of wanting to accumulate progress and have visible signs of this progress. From the time our Neanderthal ancestors were coveting their neighbours' livestock, to the modern, harried executive coveting a promotion at work, we are conditioned to work harder and exert effort when it looks like there is a prize waiting to be earned. Marketing professors Joseph Drèze from the Wharton School of Business and Joseph C. Nunes of UCLA have done a lot of research on this subject.[2] Their experiments with loyalty programmes bear out what they call 'The Endowed Progress Effect' or in their words, 'how artificial advancement increases effort'. For example, when consumers are shown that they are making headway and are on their way to achieve some milestone, they exert more effort to get there. You might recall those mailers telling you that you're just a few flights away from Gold Status, or the text messages reminding you of your point balance and how you can get elite status and the wonderful discounts it entails soon.

It is for this reason most successful loyalty programmes have very visible and aspirational signals of tiers and levels (Gold, Platinum etc.). These are also usually accompanied by visible (to both the consumer getting these benefits, and to those who are not) signals of positive reinforcement. In the airline example, one visible symbol is separate lines for check-in or prioritized boarding. Such visible perks make the progress to the next level feel more desirable.

The final ingredient is empathy. The strongest brands and best-run businesses gain loyalty by showing their customers that they are truly making an attempt to understand you as an individual. They send very visible signals to show that they are going that extra step to uniquely meet your needs. We see such empathy in action all the time, especially in small businesses. For example, the local barber who knows all about you and chats with you as he cuts your hair; the small bookstore owner who asks how the last book was and orders a new release by your favourite author.

Large businesses try and replicate that same level of personalization and empathy, and those who manage to do it, thrive. Take for example Starbucks, where baristas are trained to remember not just the names of regular customers but also sometimes the very exact specifications they have for their drinks. In its first full year in India, Starbucks outperformed its rivals—clocking revenues upwards of Rs 95 crore, and same store sales of more than twice that of its domestic rivals. Part of that success comes from how Starbucks thinks about consumer loyalty. It has developed a vocabulary of its own. Try saying the following really fast repeatedly: Venti low-fat hazelnut latte with an extra shot of coffee, half-cream and extra syrup. The rhythmic jargon works like a charm to build loyalty.

Thus Starbucks uses a simple insight to ensure loyalty. If customers feel more ownership over their drink, then they are likely to come back more often. Starbucks calls this 'mass customization' based on their experience that customers rarely ask for a plain coffee. That level of customization and consumer empathy is not something other coffee chains in India have developed yet. The other side of this, of course, is the level of training, development, perks and career prospects that Starbucks offers so that it has a far lower employee turnover rate than its rivals in India. This means that if you're a loyal Starbucks consumer, you will likely meet the same set of baristas over time, further enhancing the chance that they get to know you. In most other chains, you will likely meet a different server every month.

So, simply put, these three principles are what make a good loyalty programme work.

Positive reinforcement, visible progress and empathy. It's not rocket science.

• • •

If we take away the fact that these principles have been distilled by marketers through many years of experience in getting consumers to repeat patterns of behaviour, we would still recognize them intuitively. In fact, one could argue that almost all of us need to use these principles every single day. A fundamental part of our lives involves influencing others to act in a way which we would consider desirable and to repeat those patterns of behaviour. Having now worked in the corporate sector for two decades, I see it play out every day: Bosses trying to get their direct reports to focus on the priorities they want, and to approach issues in the way they want; on the flip side, those same reports trying to influence their bosses to repeat the behaviour they want, whether it is giving positive appraisals or promotions.

At a larger level, organizations spend a lot of time, effort and money in trying to build loyalty and performance among employees. They try to encourage desired behaviour of performing better over time and inhibiting their people from moving to another organization. In doing so, they are taking a leaf out of a marketer's book with respect to their loyalty programmes, by rewarding longer tenure with stock options that have longer vesting periods and give larger cumulative rewards over time. They also reward performance with bonuses and giving visible symbols of progress with promotions, specialized designations and enhanced responsibilities. And this approach does not just hold for people in suits in corporate boardrooms.

My father and my maternal grandfather were both in the Indian Police Service. They would tell me how they were drilled endlessly on marching, standing in attention for hours and using firearms. Repeated drills that were meant to drive home one and only one thing—absolute, non-questioning and instinctive delivery of what was required and ordered.

If someone faltered, for example, stopping while marching, there was instant negative reinforcement through extra rounds of exercise. On the other hand, if someone did well, there was positive reinforcement—a simple pat on the back or an extra ration of eggs. The empathy came from the fact that officers were expected to know each of their men intimately. They were expected to know what was on their minds, lead from the front and literally put their lives on the line for their men. The principles were in essence no different from what marketers use in encouraging consumers to act in a certain way repeatedly. This is because the basic human need is the same—to repeat what is encouraged and desist from what is discouraged.

From our families to workplaces, even at the level of nation states contending for national advantage or gain, these principles play out at every level. Sanctions are enforced when a country does something outside the boundaries of good morality expected by the international community. Aid and technology transfer flow in to help those nations who decide to comply with the desires of the international community. India faced severe sanctions from many Western powers after its 1998 nuclear weapons testing, and was forced to rely on a lot of indigenous efforts to develop its space and defence capabilities. This is part of the reason why the late president, Abdul Kalam, is held in such great esteem. A lot of our achievements in the missile and space fields were realized without the ability to simply import technology or solutions to make them happen. We had to develop a lot of the technology from scratch.

However, things began to change over the years. Economic liberalization in India kicked in and the economy began to boom; the shakiness of the alliance of convenience with Pakistan in containing terror became clearer, and China was suddenly seen as a threat and not just as a billion consumers for Western firms. India was able to offer up the major world powers the carrot of the huge Indian market and the promise of making business easier to do. This is also

encapsulated well in Modi's 3-D mantra of why India will be
so important to the rest of the world: demographic dividend,
democracy and demand from a billion plus consumers. These
same global powers have now turned a full 360 degrees. The
United States, which led the way in placing sanctions on
India back in the 1990s and questioned why India needed
nuclear weapons, has in 2015 emerged as the single largest
supplier of weapons to India.

This just goes to show that positive and negative
reinforcement can work both ways. Those who are the recipients
of negative reinforcement, as India was for years, can change the
conversation by offering their own positive reinforcement. In
doing so, the Indian government is also smartly building off its
own version of a 'loyalty programme'. It is incentivizing foreign
suppliers with preferential treatment and larger orders if they
agree to set up technology transfers or manufacturing in India
under the banner of 'Make in India'. The same companies that
twenty years ago would not dream of supplying to India due
to sanctions imposed by their governments, are now jockeying
for contracts. The pressure to create jobs back in their own
countries is in turn leading those governments to relax a lot
of the constraints that had once existed in doing business with
India in the fields of defence and space.

• • •

Now, let's try and apply these principles of building
consumer loyalty to yet another everyday challenge. This is

to do with something that plays out in homes every single day. The fundamental task is the same. Getting someone to repeat patterns of desirable behaviour and avoid behaviour we would consider undesirable.

I'm speaking of parents trying to get their children to behave in a way they want them to.

If we were to apply the learning from Skinner, Drèze, the many others who have followed them and indeed, the accumulated experience of countless companies around the world, one would conclude that the same principles that go into a loyalty programme should work in reinforcing positive behaviour among our children too, right? Instead, it's instructional to see how Indian parents actually try and get their children to do what they want.

First, let's take positive reinforcement. Far from positively reinforcing desired behaviour, the vast majority of Indian parents seem to favour negative punishment as a means to threaten kids into doing what they want. An early 2015 study by Bornsmart, a parenting organization, showed that 62 per cent of parents in Mumbai said that they hit their children. Professor Skinner would probably have told these parents that giving a shock to his rat would not have gotten them to do the desired activity like pressing a lever, but have the opposite effect instead.

In Skinner's experiments, negative reinforcement actually made the animal withdraw. Which is why a child being harangued and beaten for not doing homework will not suddenly see the light and attack homework with gusto,

but more often than not, develop negative associations with
it. Not that it helps the parents either. In the same study,
23 per cent of parents felt guilty about hitting the child and
brought them a gift, thereby totally confusing the message;
26 per cent said 'sorry' and 28 per cent cried with the child.
If you were a marketer trying to get your consumer to do
something, blaming them for not buying your brand on
their previous trip to the supermarket through an abusive
email written in ALL CAPS, and then following up with a
discount voucher would sound absurd and achieve only one
thing—a consumer who never buys your product again. And
yet, that's what the study shows most parents do.

Wouldn't it be better if instead we embraced positive
reinforcement, encouraged our children to work on things
that we believe are going to help them and then reward them?
This way, our children will see the positive impact of the
things we want them to do. And I'm not talking of bribing
a child with expensive gifts or toys every time she does her
homework or behaves well. Given the current environment
where nearly two in three parents are hitting their kids,
perhaps a meaningful reward is just to spend quality time
with your child. You could read a book with him or her,
order a favourite choice of food, watch cartoons with them
etc. In the context of parenting, sharing your child's world
with them is perhaps the most important reward a parent
can offer. It's much harder work than smacking a child when
she does not behave or palming her off to the maid because
you're too busy. It requires patience, and as any marketer

will tell you, building a brand takes time and patience. Why should parenting be any easier?

Second, let's get to visible progress. Imagine a loyalty programme where the communication to you says that you have accumulated fewer points than your neighbour and hence you are not going to get to the next tier while he will. How would you feel? Insulted? Angry? Of course, and that's why all loyalty programmes don't compare you to others negatively. They focus on the progress you've made and what you need to do to move on to the next tier or level, and the positives you can expect from said progress. However, in many homes, what parents do to encourage progress is to compare their child with others. How many of us have grown up hearing about 'Mrs Sharma's (insert the name as appropriate) prodigal son who got x per cent marks or a certain rank'? So many companies have figured out that what works to motivate desired behaviour is showcasing progress and measuring where *you* are versus *yourself*.

Wouldn't it be a far more motivational journey for the child to have a board up in their room where he or she is rewarded with a star for doing something good? Every time a certain number of stars are reached, the child is treated to something positive. This approach of visualizing and encouraging progress and positively reinforcing progress perhaps may motivate a child to strive to achieve more of the positive 'strokes' than any number of haranguing comparisons made with the neighbours' prodigal child. This is essentially what brands also do.

The final piece is that of empathy, of truly striving to understand our children and guiding and motivating them to achieve their potential and fulfil their dreams and aspirations. That also sounds like common sense, right? Data would suggest otherwise.

A survey titled 'The Value of Education—Learning for Life' was conducted by HSBC Bank in early 2015, covering the attitudes of parents in nine different countries on several parameters related to what they wanted for their children. The results, as reported in the *Wall Street Journal* in July 2015 are telling.[3]

Per Cent Agreeing to What They Want Most For Their Children	Fulfil Their Potential	Be Healthy	Be Happy	Be Successful in Career
Rank 1	UK (50)	China (72)	Canada (78)	India (51)
Rank 2	Canada (45)	Hong Kong (39)	UK (77)	UAE (43)
Rank 3	US (40)	Australia (34)	Australia (77)	Brazil (32)
Rank 4	Australia (40)	US (33)	US (72)	Canada (24)

Rank 5	Hong Kong (33)	Canada (33)	China (63)	US (21)
Rank 6	China (26)	**India (33)**	Brazil (62)	Hong Kong (19)
Rank 7	**India (17)**	Brazil (30)	UAE (60)	UK (17)
Rank 8	UAE (15)	UAE (29)	Hong Kong (58)	Australia (17)
Rank 9	Brazil (13)	UK (27)	**India (49)**	China (15)

I'm sure the patriot in each of us would be happy to see India at the top of a list, but in this case, I'm not too sure. Indian parents are at the top when it comes to wanting kids to be successful in their careers. But they are near the bottom of the list on others, and the absolute last when it comes to wanting kids to be happy. That tells us something.

It tells us that while we as parents focus on career success as we define it for our kids, we are far less bothered about how they get there and how that leaves them feeling.

No wonder most Indian parents pack kids off to coaching classes to get them into the assembly line of IITs or other entrance exams without checking to see if that is something the child has any interest in or aptitude for. A poorly designed loyalty programme will result in lost sales and customers. While we would like to believe that our kids do not have the luxury of opting out, the data released by the education ministry illustrates how wrong that assumption is. Recently, the number of students dropping out from IITs has steadily increased from 606 in 2012–13 to 757 in 2013–14, with the largest stated cause being 'pressure'. An even more extreme form of this pressure shows in the rising suicides among IIT and medical aspirants in Kota. Over the last few years, Kota has emerged as a 'coaching centre hub' for such aspirants with more than forty major coaching centres and close to 1.25 lakh students enrolling each year. The intense pressure (both academic and societal), the lack of any family support system and the fact that many of these kids are here without much consideration for where their aptitude and desire really lie is beginning to take a real and terrible toll on the youth. In 2015, thirty of these students chose to end their own lives, committing suicide instead of continuing to toil in the pressure-cooker environment they had found themselves in.

There is another side to this picture. Kids in school may not be able to think through for themselves what they really want to do and run around in the Skinner's Box created by parents and peer pressure. However, when they are able to think through what they truly want to do, they will opt out. Studies show that almost 90 per cent of IIT graduates are working in fields that have no relation to engineering and up to 60 per cent of them go on to study business management. So essentially, when they are able to do so, they will opt out.

Marketers spend hours with their consumers trying to understand them and their motivations, in addition to spending lots of money on market research to glean what is on their consumers' minds, in order to come up with loyalty programmes that will resonate with them. As a parent, we don't need to hire a research agency, or spend any research money, or sit in focus groups or look at research reports. We just need to sit with our children and seek to understand what it is they truly aspire to do, and discuss how we can help them achieve their potential.

It's certain that there is no easy way to turn off the switch of misplaced parental pressure and expectations. But I hope this chapter helps each of us think about the principles not just of marketing, but of fundamental human behaviour and motivations. These principles underpin the methods used by marketers to generate desired behaviour and loyalty among consumers. Using those same principles in our own homes could potentially lead to much more productive engagement with our children. By creating this environment, our children will not feel pressured to meet someone else's definition of success. Also, they will feel understood and encouraged to develop their potential further. The genesis of our modern understanding of the psychology behind this may come from the experiments Skinner performed with rats in his boxes, but perhaps it is time we stopped treating our kids as lab rats and liberated them from the rat race. At stake is something much more fundamental and lasting than annual sales targets or brand equity scores. At stake is our future generation.

• • •

THE THREE MANTRAS OF THE SHASTRA OF LOYALTY

- Spare the rod, incentivize the child. Don't use negative reinforcement as a means to get someone to do something you consider desirable. Chances are you'll get the opposite result. Instead focus on rewarding desired behaviour, whether it is in your child, employee or significant other.

- Even if you think life is a race, you'll be most motivated when you're racing against yourself. Don't negatively compare yourself and others you're trying to incentivize. People stretch and perform much better when they can see themselves improving, not by being compared unfavourably to others.

- Loyalty begins with empathy. Make a genuine attempt to understand what success is for those you're trying to impact, and build off that, instead of foisting your definition of success on them. Whether at home, with friends, or at the workplace, that will serve you well.

5

The Shastra of Habit Change

Introducing the New, Improved You

The last three chapters were about some of the foundational challenges faced by every marketer. To remind you, in marketing jargon these are creating differentiation, trial and repeat. In layman language, it's about setting your brand apart in the consumer's mind from other choices they have (differentiation). It's about making a consumer try your brand when they are using some other (trial), and then getting them to come back to your brand and become loyal to it (repeat). These quests occupy a large part of many marketers' waking hours, but there is still one quest that is perhaps even tougher and takes longer to achieve.

This challenge is trying to bring about a change in consumer habits. By doing this, the marketer is trying to get the consumer from not using a category altogether to start using it. By its very definition, this is harder than getting a consumer to switch from one brand to another, since the consumer has perhaps not even tried the category you are playing in before. An example of this could be trying to make a mother who is using cloth diapers switch to disposable diapers, or to convince someone who has never ordered anything online to use an e-commerce site, or getting a small business to use your firm's services to set up a website when it has never had an online presence before. Thus it is much harder work for a marketer than just getting a consumer to switch from one brand to another since the consumer is unaware of the new category altogether. There is no magic bullet to achievement here and there are also nuances in every category. But there are some broad principles marketers have learned and outlined over the years on what it takes to get consumers to change habits. I'll discuss these now.

First, instead of just focusing on what product or category the consumer is using today (the current habit), focus on the consumer's underlying need this product or habit satisfies.

What marketers have learned is that instead of just focusing on the exhibited behaviour (the habit), it is equally important to understand and focus on why that habit exists and what needs it satisfies. Indeed, in the bestselling book, *The Power of Habit*, Charles Duhigg argues that the focus on habit change is often misplaced, but instead what is often required is finding a new way of meeting an underlying need, which will continue to be there even if the habit changes. A couple of examples bring this reasoning to life. Despite spending a fair amount of money, e-commerce firms in India found it hard going at first. The focus on habit change would lead them to talk of variety and convenience, since on the face of it, these were the most 'tangible' benefits of this new habit compared to how Indian consumers have traditionally shopped. But the real need that had to be met was of the consumer desiring to stay in control and play safe when it came to making payments online. Indian consumers wanted to ensure they got the product before they paid for it. Moreover, most Indian consumers were used to paying in cash, also in part because they felt it to be 'safer' and awarding more control in their hands, so purely 'importing' a Western model of credit card based payments limited the appeal of initial forays in the e-commerce space in India. Several sites experimented with cash on delivery and then Flipkart took it 'mainstream' by announcing a cash-on-delivery option in 2010. Consumers could now feel more in control of the transaction and see and touch the goods they had ordered before paying. That in part led to the explosion of e-commerce in India and even today, well over half of all online transactions in India are cash on delivery.

Another good example is how Cadbury in India inserted itself into the traditional gifting space. Historically chocolates were seen as a treat for children, but Cadbury was able to establish itself into this important consumption occasion by tapping into the basic need (spreading happiness) and also cleverly identified cues (such as chocolates with fruits and nuts, traditionally given for gifting, and packaging that borrowed cues from traditional mithai packaging) which would reassure consumers that they weren't going too far from what was traditionally associated with the occasion. The functional need of a sweet gift was met, as was the underlying need of this being associated with traditional festivals like Diwali—as it was important for many customers to maintain a strong link with tradition.

Moving on, a second way to switch consumer habits is not to harp on what is wrong with the current habit, but instead focus on the positives of the new habit. Once consumers have an established habit, focusing on the negative can be dangerous. Far from getting them to adopt a new habit, it can backfire as it may alienate consumers by making them look bad and telling them that the choices they have made are bad. One such campaign was kicked off by Colgate as far back as the late 1970s. While Colgate was already the market leader in India, it realized there was huge opportunity in getting more people to use toothpaste. At the time, less than half the population used toothpaste. Talking about dental hygiene went some distance. The biggest barrier was being clear on what the benefits of using toothpaste versus traditional dental care routines (powders, herbs) was. This was not easy to explain when people said that they had been using the same dental hygiene routine for years, and so had their parents. The breakthrough came when Colgate began talking about the positive payoffs of using toothpaste instead of just comparing it to traditional routines. Colgate started running a campaign where brushing regularly unlocked greater intimacy between husband and wife. It then started a campaign in schools where healthy teeth were linked to success and staying in school. In more modern times, marketers of disposable diapers have taken a leaf out of the same book. From talking about the fact that babies cannot sleep as well when they are uncomfortable with traditional cloth covering, marketers like P&G's Pampers team have taken it to the next level by talking about how uninterrupted sleep is linked to a child's overall development. A consumer may rationalize a bit of wetness as no big thing, especially as previous generations have passed on the habit. But few mothers can resist something that tells them about how their child can develop better.

Third, be patient and set milestones, and not just one absolute end goal. The reality is that habit change takes time, because any established way of doing things has its own inertia. Going back to the e-commerce example, e-commerce firms spent more than Rs 3000 crore on advertising in 2015 and the category is booming, growing at well over 50 per cent year on year. In 2015, it was estimated that the e-commerce market was about $16 billion in size. The numbers sound huge, but it is just over 2 per cent of the total retail market in India. All that money spent, all that effort, and clearly the habit of shopping has changed only for a small minority. That would be the glass half-empty view of things, if one had set a very short-term goal. The marketers and investors in e-commerce are of course taking a long-term view and are making investments with that sort of perspective. They are comforted by the fact that e-commerce is growing at more than seven to eight times the growth rate of the overall retail market. And going back to the Colgate example, in mid-2014, the Colgate India managing director said in a media interview that while in urban India its penetration among consumers was 90 per cent, in rural India it was 63 per cent. Three decades of disseminating a message and still more than one third of rural Indian consumers don't get it? Again, the glass half-full view is that penetration has increased by more than 50 per cent from mid-1970s' levels in rural India and slowly, but surely, changes in habit are happening.

And finally, recruit allies to help consumers get over the perceived risk of adopting a new habit. When Colgate uses the

Indian Dental Association to talk of the benefits of brushing or Dettol wheels out a man in a white coat talking about how the Indian Medical Association endorses the antiseptic, they are both doing the same thing. Their marketers are trying to use allies in helping consumers adopt their message. The biggest barrier that often comes in the way of consumers adopting a new habit is the risk associated with trying something new, unfamiliar and different from the routine they are used to and comfortable with. What if there are side effects because the toothpaste has chemicals? What if I order the product from the website but the product doesn't get delivered? What if my baby gets a rash from the diaper? These allies need not just be medical associations or men in white coats. Sometimes the biggest source of reassurance is 'someone like me', who says that the new habit is 'right'. This is why many marketers use consumer testimonials as a tool. Whisper is a good example of this. The company advocated the benefits of using a sanitary pad versus cloth, which was traditionally used, by a woman talking in the first person of how it benefited her, instead of a scientific sale on product benefits alone.

• • •

That's enough about how marketers go about getting consumers to change habits. The reality is that all of us, in our daily lives, do confront the task of changing habits—of those around us, or of ourselves. I remember as a child I would keep asking my father not to smoke, but it was his habit, formed when he himself was little more than a child. At that time I had no way of knowing or understanding that he had taken up smoking to help cope with the trauma of the Partition and of having to start afresh in a new home in India. And at that time, I had no understanding of the concepts I outlined above, but I began to ask him to cut down smoking as I didn't want to lose him; I had read and heard in school that smoking killed people. I had formulated my request in the innocence of childhood, without perhaps understanding exactly what I was saying. My father had lost his father when he was less than ten years old. Perhaps my telling him that I didn't want to lose him triggered a change in his habit. From a chain-smoker, he gradually cut down to the point where he stopped altogether. Years later, I saw the power of habit changes in my own life. I started drinking heavily to cope with my mother's death to cancer. At one point, I weighed 98 kilos. When my wife came into my life, I began to realize that I had been drinking to protest the unfairness of it all. Perhaps I was punishing myself for not being able to do anything to help my mother. In other words, I recognized the underlying need I was trying to fill with my habit. With my wife in my life, and so much to look forward to, I began to focus on the positives, and found a replacement for drinking—running. If there were negative thoughts in my head, I found that sweating them off after a hard run helped me deal with them much better (and with less damage to myself) than drinking. I monitored progress— not on weight, since I knew that was just an outcome. But

I monitored how much I ran every day. I went from 98 to 72 kilos in just over a year, and even today, more than ten years later, my weight hovers around 73 kilos. When people who knew me back then ask me how I lost so much weight, I say flippantly, 'drink less, run more'. But the reality is that I achieved it by applying many of the principles I had been using in my day job as a marketer to get consumers to change their habits and embrace new ways of doing things.

The principles of changing habits or acquiring a new habit also play out on a much broader canvas, beyond such individual changes, for example, changes that span a nation or indeed, the whole world. Some of you may not be old enough to have seen these ads for yourself, but I'm sure most of you will recall the jingle, *'Sunday ho ya Monday, roz khao ande'*. The National Egg Coordination Council kicked off the campaign in the mid-1980s to increase egg consumption in India. This was done both to give a boost to the poultry industry and also to enhance the nutritional value of what average Indians consumed. The campaign had most of the elements of any successful habit change exercise—they showcased the benefits of consuming eggs, linking it to a specific ritual or measurable habit (one a day). They used the power of endorsement very well. To an average consumer, it seemed to be coming from a government (related) body as opposed to a private company or lobby. They also used popular figures like Dara Singh, whom consumers would readily associate with the health benefits being talked about.

There were several underlying factors beyond the campaign that contributed to the end results, such as the impact of changing lifestyles and urbanization on food habits. However, the bottom line was that between 1980 and 2000, while overall agricultural production increased by 1.5 to 2 per cent per annum, egg consumption increased by 8 to 10 per cent per annum.

Other efforts, aimed at breaking even more entrenched habits and prejudices, may need more time. One such multifaceted effort is the campaign, led by the government and non-government organizations (NGOs), to reduce the birth rate in India, especially in rural areas. One leg of the effort is focused on the adoption of birth control methods and talks about the economic advantages of having smaller families. Another parallel effort is trying to tackle the root cause of a high birth rate, which is that many families continue trying to have children till they have a son, a deeply held preference among many Indian families. A campaign of this nature will not have as fast a result as a campaign to get parents to use diapers or toothpaste, because here what is being dealt with are not just perceptions and attitudes to products of a particular category, but some of the basic assumptions and mores that go into the making of our society. Many NGOs and government agencies work tirelessly to spread education, awareness and also a healthy dose of negative reinforcement where needed. We see a lot of visible communication around sex determination tests and female infanticide. By doing this, they are trying to change some of the terrible habits that underlie both our declining ratio of girls to boys and the still-high population growth rates.

• • •

Let's now apply some of this understanding about changing habits to something that most of us have grappled with at some point or the other in our lives. This is something that perhaps all of us have committed ourselves to do, and even perhaps failed to do it.

I'm talking about sticking to our New Year resolutions.

Making New Years' resolutions seems to be a universal phenomenon. According to surveys done in the United States by the University of Scranton, around 40 to 50 per cent of its population makes resolutions each year.[1] However, keeping those resolutions is quite another matter. Research by the University of Scranton shows that a paltry 8 per cent of people actually manage to reach the goals they set for themselves with these resolutions. I'm sure you at some point or the other have made resolutions too, as have I. However, if I can make a guess, most of the time these resolutions have remained statements of positive intent, having been fuelled by celebratory spirits on New Year's Eve. I know I personally have been guilty of making a resolution which I've broken just a few days later, and there are many friends and relatives I know who have done the same. So if you've made resolutions and not been able to stick to them, don't feel guilty. You are in good company, and from what marketers have learned over the years, it is never easy to change any habit.

But what can the learning on habit change teach us about getting better at keeping our resolutions? Let's first understand what the most common resolutions made in India are. A survey by NDTV in early 2015, based on over 7000 respondents, identified the most common New Year resolutions as the following:

#1 Resolution	Per Cent Respondents
Lose weight and get fitter	56.61
Less stress; better work–life balance	20.38
Let people I care about know how I feel	11.53
Watch less TV and read more	6.65

What is clear about the resolutions is that most of them are about changing the status quo. Stopping something and starting something else. Doing less of something and more of something else. In other words, changing habits. What is also clear from the survey is that Indians are no different from Americans when it comes to the inability to keep these resolutions. Forty per cent of the respondents said that they had an urge to break the resolution in the first week itself and just 30 per cent were able to keep to their resolution for more than a month.

What if the researchers at NDTV had also monitored how many people actually stuck to their resolutions over the long-term? While that data is not captured in the survey, I imagine it would have been in single digits, similar to the US survey. These numbers by themselves should not be shocking. As the first part of this chapter shows, changing any habit is hard work. Stopping anything that you have done for years, something that has become not just a part of your routine but indeed a part of your personality, is hard to do.

So let's take each of the marketing principles we discussed earlier in this chapter and see how they might be applied to our resolutions and potential habit changes. The first is to focus on and understand our underlying need, not just the habit in itself. The most common reason people have a weight problem (picking the #1 resolution in the above poll) is usually simple as far as habits go—eating unhealthy food and not getting enough exercise. However, a broad resolution of wanting to lose weight without getting into the real needs these current habits serve is not likely to work. This is because unless another way is found to meet those underlying needs, the tendency to lapse into old habits will be very strong. A clear linkage has been found between emotional states and overeating. Beat, a leading charity for eating disorders in the United Kingdom, through its work with the Emotional Overeating Support Group, a project funded by the Department of Health, found that 87.6 per cent of people overeat because of emotional reasons and to cope with issues like loneliness, stress or anxiety. We've all heard the phrase 'comfort food', and can all identify with binging once in a while when we felt terrible about something. This data should make us all feel a bit better—we are far from alone. So just saying you want to or will lose weight does not count for much if the next time you have a bad day at the office or a tiff with the girlfriend, you reach for a package of chips and some beer. Oh yes, that makes things even worse, since research in the UK (commissioned by Slimming World with YouGov, as reported in the BBC's Health Section on 24 April 2014) has shown that when you drink too much, you significantly increase the chances of overeating.[2] According to the study, people who drink more than three glasses of wine consume on average an extra 6300 calories over the next twenty-four hours. So if losing weight is on your mind, as it seems to be for so many Indians, don't focus on the habit of eating, but look at how you intend to replace eating junk or overeating as the solution for those stress points. Instead of an abstract desire to eat less junk food, identify those moments (for example, after a long meeting, after a long day at work, after an argument) when there is an emotional need to eat and find a substitute. Also, consciously plan exercise in such a way that it a part of your day. Don't just take my word for it. The University of East Anglia and the Centre for Diet and Activity Research in the United Kingdom studied eighteen years of data across 18,000 people and published their results in 2014. The study explored multiple aspects of psychological health. It concluded that simple walking can significantly reduce stress. So if losing weight is on your mind, be clear on where and when you feel most stressed and then make a conscious effort to associate those moments with doing some physical activity. Even just taking a simple, short walk (preferably where junk food is not within arm's reach) and you're likely to make more progress than a broad proclamation of eating healthier or losing weight.

The second principle is to focus on the positives, not the absence of a negative. To start, take how most people phrase their resolutions. If we look at the survey above, the top resolutions are negative—losing weight, less pressure etc. But marketers who have led habit change programmes will tell you that it is always better to focus on the positives of the new routine, instead of the negatives of the old. In the context of weight loss, it can be as simple as fitting into some clothes you've always wanted to wear. The jury is still out on this and experts would caution against setting unrealistic goals (see the next point). Nonetheless, there is some evidence that seeing yourself as fitting into desirable clothes as a motivator or a reward can help push one forward into weight loss, by giving a tangible and positive payoff.

In an online survey done on the popular online weight loss support community, 3fatchicks.com in September 2012, among those who had successfully reached their target weight, 51 per cent of respondents said they had bought clothes smaller in size as a motivational tool. Also, around 48 per cent rewarded themselves for losing weight by buying new clothes they had always wanted to fit into. So whether it's losing weight or taking on less work-related stress, you should focus on the positive outcomes.

And if you're someone who spends a lot of time at work and wants to get more balance (the #2 resolution in India according to the NDTV survey), don't just make a resolution of getting out of the office at six in the evening every day. You may well find that you were spending that time in the office because you had nothing else to replace it with. Even if you get out of the office at six, without a more attractive alternative, you may find yourself thinking about work, answering emails and soon, getting back into the old habit of staying late. On the other hand, if you plan outings with friends and family, or join classes in the evening to pursue a hobby or learn something new, you will have something positive to look forward to. This would fill the gap that leaving the office early gives you in your routine.

The third principle is to set milestones, not just think of some absolute end goal. Marketers who have worked on changing consumer habits will tell you that patience is critical. Instead of setting a long-range goal which inevitably leads to disappointment, it's better to set lots of interim goals and monitor and track progress. In the case of weight loss, to take that analogy forward, the lesson learned would be not to make a brave proclamation of 'I'll lose 10 kilos by my next birthday' but instead to break it up into bite-sized chunks. For example, a couple of kilos in a couple of months, or even better, to use the previous lesson, fit into jeans one size smaller in a couple of months. There is a fair bit of research that backs this up as well. A study conducted by the University of Iowa, quoted in the *Oxford Journal of Health Education Research*, showed that a higher frequency of goal setting correlated very highly with achieving goals related to both diet and physical activity.

That brings me to the fourth and final point—seeking allies. In the case of changing habits, sometimes the simplest way of finding an 'ally' is not running to someone in a white coat, but just sharing it with someone close to you. That increases the stakes, makes your commitment more public and also gets people involved who will cheer you on and keep you honest. In a study on quitting smoking, researchers found that something as simple as being part of a social media group on 'giving up smoking' significantly increased the chances of someone actually quitting. This is an example of where social media can be a friend. Announce your goals to friends, and share progress. Their encouragement will keep you going and if you do feel like you're not keeping up, you have people who can help you stay on track. And it need not necessarily be faraway friends on social media. Perhaps the most powerful ally you can find is someone very close and important to you—a best friend, a spouse, a partner. Once your resolution becomes less of lonely drudgery than something you're trying to do with a group of like-minded friends or with the support of someone who matters to you, it will all suddenly seem much easier. The logic is the same as when people who want to take up running join a running group and those training for a marathon find people to train with them.

Thus whatever your resolution, hang in there and spare a thought for the marketers who toiled for decades to change consumer habits. Tap into their learning and accumulated experience and you may well find yourself fitting into that new pair of jeans faster than you may have thought.

• • •

THE THREE MANTRAS OF THE SHASTRA OF HABIT CHANGE

- Don't focus on the 'what' but ask 'why'. It's not just behaviour that needs to be changed—you also need to understand the reason why the behaviour exists if you want to find an alternative way of meeting that need.
- It's not always about being the 'Biggest Loser'— don't focus on the absence of a negative, but on what positive things will be part of your life once you make the switch.
- Make it social. Get friends or people you trust in on the change you want to make, and get their support to help you.

6
The Shastra of Celebrity Endorsement

Lessons in Adding Glamour to Your Résumé

I THOUGHT WE WERE HIRING FOR AN ENGINEER. HIS REFEREES READ LIKE THE CAST OF A BOLLYWOOD BLOCKBUSTER.

They are all around us. They seem to have a passionate point of view on everything from underwear to paan masala. They seduce, cajole and convince us to join them in adopting the object of their affections. We follow them on Twitter, we like them on Facebook and many people line up outside their homes just to get a glimpse of them. They lead very public lives.

Yes, I'm talking about celebrities.

It is a cliché that India is a celebrity mad country. While it's hard to say if the craze for celebrities is higher or lower than other countries, our obsession with celebrities, often literally elevating them to divine status with temples dedicated to them, is pretty unique. Indian marketers certainly seem to embrace celebrities in selling their brands. While the explosion of channels (both more TV channels and the emergence of digital) and more consumerism means we see their endorsements more often, using celebrities to build brands is hardly a new phenomenon.

Even back in the 1970s and early 1980s, when all we had to watch on the idiot box was Doordarshan and multimedia advertising for marketers meant a radio spot or a print ad, celebrities were a favoured means of plugging brands. From Amjad Khan holding aloft a pack of Glucon D proclaiming the biscuits were '*Gabbar ki asli pasand*', to Vinod Khanna taking beachside rides on his horse while sharing his bathing soap preferences, 'I use Cinthol, do you?', and to a procession of stars lounging in bathtubs courtesy Lux, since the early days, celebrities have been a staple part of the marketer's arsenal.

AdEx India, a media research powerhouse, shows that just between 2003 and 2007, celebrity use in advertising rose 7.45 times. A seven-fold increase in just four years! Given the exorbitant fees many top celebrities charge, one may wonder why and how marketers use them on such a scale. The reason is simple—on the whole, using celebrities works.

There are many studies on the subject, but to take one conducted in the Indian context, a study by professors Anjum, Dhanda and Nagra, published in the *Asia Pacific Journal of Marketing & Management Review* in October 2012,[1] showed the clear positive connotations Indian consumers linked with celebrity advertising. In other words, the analysis they presented showed the positive associations consumers form when celebrities are used to endorse a brand. In this study, the highest ratings were given to the statements 'Celebrity endorsers are more reliable', 'Celebrity endorsers are more knowledgeable than regular endorsers' and 'Celebrities ensure high degree of recall'. The net result: If you want your brand to stand out in the clutter and establish a positive image for your brand in the consumer's mind, using celebrities is a pretty good way to go.

Right?

Well, maybe.

That's because using celebrities is a tool, and like any tool, its utility and impact depends on *how* it is used. So, what have marketers learned over the years on how best to use celebrities?

As a foundational principle, marketers advise the use of a celebrity whose personality and imagery matches your brand and then use them strategically to build your brand. Don't use them simply because they are well known or popular. In marketing lingo, marketers think of 'brand personality' or 'brand character', which refer to the set of associations they want to create with their brand. Often they start with the question, 'if my brand were to be a person, how would I want consumers to describe it?' When the celebrity being chosen to endorse a brand amplifies and complements that particular brand character, there can be a clear positive pay off. Vinod Khanna worked beautifully with the rugged, masculine and confident imagery Cinthol was trying to project at the time. Using Sachin Tendulkar and other sports stars seemed a natural move for Boost, which talked of being energetic. To take another example, Akshay Kumar seemed a great fit with Thums Up and its masculine, adventurous imagery. In all cases, the celebrity helped enhance the point of difference for the brand (see Chapter 2), which helps set it apart from other brands. When the celebrity in some ways embodies the brand, it's perhaps the most powerful way to use a celebrity to build the brand.

However, some marketers go astray in using celebrities as wallpaper, especially when they use them because they are well known or have a pretty face, with little thought to how they fit with their brand. A Bollywood starlet might well enhance the appeal for a brand of lipstick, since that is clearly part of what she may be seen as credibly using to enhance her own appearance and appeal. But her endorsement for a brand of paan masala may leave one scratching one's head. Indeed, sometimes the brands that stand out and make an impact are the ones which actually don't follow the herd. Dove in beauty care is a good example. Instead of joining other brands which all used celebrities, it uses real women as part of a broader positioning of 'real beauty' to create a very distinctive space for itself in the category.

Second, if you're using a celebrity, watch out for credibility issues. It is very tempting for a marketer to use a celebrity and one does sometimes hear excitable conversations about how the new celebrity will get the brand to be the talk of the town. An old friend of mine at an advertising agency would tell me stories of how his client, the promoter at a large firm, would hand him a suitcase filled with cash and say, '*Koi acchi si film star daal do ad mein*'. Such a fixation with stars and celebrities is indeed a reality in our society, and marketers are no different when it comes to be being besotted with stars. In 2012, according to data from AdEx, 83.2 per cent of ads which used celebrities had film actors and actresses (the split being almost equal between them), with the balance almost entirely made up of sports figures. If you get the feeling that you sometimes see the same celebrity endorsing every brand you can think of, there is a basis for that. According to the same data, in 2010, the three most-used celebrities endorsed sixty-nine brands between them during those twelve months.

This is a mind-boggling number. On average, each of these three celebrities was the face for over twenty brands. Truth is if you're going to be endorsing so many brands, it's little surprise that those categories are as diverse as cement and bikes; energy drinks and fairness creams.

Still, using celebrities does have its benefits. But the problem for marketers is that as consumers, we're all a bit smarter than they give us credit for. Of course, we like looking at good-looking celebrities, but we are savvy enough to figure out when the celebrity isn't really using the brand in question. That can seriously hurt the credibility of the brand and sometimes be counterproductive. The study which appeared in the *Asia Pacific Journal* mentioned that the biggest negative factor in brand appeal came when 'celebrities were endorsing one brand and using another'.

A high-profile recent example of credibility issues would be Amitabh Bachchan publicly saying that he would stop endorsing Pepsi. Bachchan was associated with the brand for many years but decided to stop after a little girl asked him why he endorsed a drink that was 'poison'. Let's put the legalities aside for a moment—the contractual obligations between Mr Bachchan and Pepsi are best known to them. Also, let's ignore our personal points of view on colas. But, from a marketer's perspective, this was nothing short of a nightmare. To a typical Indian consumer who regards Mr Bachchan with a high level of respect and admiration, his expressing a point of view, positive or negative, about a brand, can have a major impact.

Lastly, when you use a celebrity to endorse your brand, in a very real way you are linking your brand's fortunes to theirs. If something happens to shake consumers' faith and credibility in them, then your brand can, and often will, be affected. That's when the proliferation of TV channels looking for the latest scoop and a corresponding explosion on social media can backfire. Among recent global examples are Tiger Woods and Lance Armstrong, who were the face of many major brands. Billions of dollars of sales were riding on their endorsements and credibility. When scandals hit them, in the case of Woods with his alleged affairs and infidelity and with Armstrong the allegations of doping, we all saw the sad spectacle of brands rushing to cut associations with them in the face of the media and public backlash.

To be fair, in many cases a marketer cannot predict what will happen and what skeletons may be lurking in a celebrity's closet. But it is important to do the right due diligence and understand the celebrity's background and also have the right legal protection in place in case things go wrong. In this day and age of social media, when a marketer signs on a celebrity, part of that due diligence is to stay connected with what's being said about the celebrity and whether there are any negative associations to watch out for. To be honest, there are few cases where this has led to lasting damage to brands. In both the Woods and Armstrong cases, the brands and causes they were associated with are none the worse for wear in the long haul. In part this is because they were quick to react and did not try and defend their endorsers in the face of public scandal and criticism. In the Indian context, the issues need not only be scandal, but the fact that fans and the media are fickle and someone who is 'hot' one day can be the target of scorn the next.

• • •

While not many of us need to call upon the services of Big B or one of the Khans to endorse our products or services, all of us at one point or the other need the endorsement or recommendation of others to refine our market offering. Any of us who has ever changed a job knows that the hiring company will ask for referees to endorse us. Very few Indian marriages (especially the arranged kind) happen without reference checks about the prospective bride or groom. Going back to the example of the differentiated groom, even the best matrimonial ad will hardly be enough, especially in the Indian social setting. This is why the private investigation business for checking matrimonial references is booming. There are around 15,000 such companies across India, conducting an average of 50–100 investigations a month during peak wedding season, according to Kumar Vikram Singh, chairman of the Association of Private Detectives of India (APDI).[2] That amounts to 1,000,000 active cases during this period, a growth of 300 per cent in the past five years, he says. Weddings are big business, and checking credentials and references before the wedding is clearly big business as well.

Endorsers can take various forms and can be found in places you might find surprising. Growing up in Delhi with my father in the government, one word that was quite widespread in government circles was *sifarish*. My father would have been tickled pink if he knew I was mentioning him in the same chapter as gym-sculpted (and Photoshopped) celebrities. For many in those days, a government officer or a minister was an 'endorser' of much use. Yes, sifarish does have connotations of bribery or impropriety. My father would often vent about how rotten much of the system was, but in the days before economic liberalization and the profusion of opportunities, it often meant a simple vote of confidence or validation of the merits of the proposal. Sometimes just moving files ahead through the bureaucratic system needed commendation from the right people. In other words, this was an endorsement that the person or the proposal on the minister or secretary's table was worthy of being approved. In those days of the Licence Raj, if you wanted to do business or get opportunities in the official machinery, you needed to call upon a very different set of celebrity endorsers. These were middle-aged officials wearing safari suits. During one of his stints, my father was the officer on special duty at the information and broadcasting ministry in the early 1990s. Given that in those days all serials aired on Doordarshan had to be approved by the I&B ministry, the ministry played an important role in clearing proposals for new serials. Being around the ministry was a good way to meet producers and directors who had proposals they wanted to clear, and indeed meet upcoming actors and actresses who were working their way into the spotlight through these serials. In later years, my father would chuckle at how far some of those actors had gone in becoming superstars and those who one day looked for endorsement from government officials were now endorsing, and driving the fortunes of, huge businesses and brands.

Of course, endorsements and the important role they play pan out on a much bigger canvas as well. When it comes to geopolitics, the ultimate endorser is the United Nations. Anyone who has seen recent history unfold on the news will see how before launching any intervention, the United States or other major global powers will often seek out some sort of approval from the UN. Not that anyone would otherwise be able to stop the major powers from intervening in Iraq or Libya, but this implicit or sometimes explicit endorsement from the United Nations is what world powers look for to justify their actions as being in line with international law, and thus above reproach.

•••

Now, let's apply this learning to an area of our everyday lives where we are often seeking to enhance our own appeal by taking an endorsement from someone. In other words, when we offer up references as part of a job application.

If you've ever applied for a job or known someone who has gone through the process (and between those two conditions, that would pretty much cover anyone reading this book), you will know that an essential part of the process is serving up references. To some people, that ends up being a mechanical process. They think in terms of, 'let me think of a couple of people whom I've worked with in the past.' Before even talking about the lessons learned in this chapter, go back to the tale of the differentiated groom in Chapter 2. When you're applying for a job, you're not just offering up passive information about yourself hoping the hiring manager discovers your skills. You're actively trying to differentiate yourself from other candidates who may well have similar educational qualifications and experiences. That's where, like a celebrity endorsement, a well-thought choice of referee can make a big difference. Or not. Because, if not thought through well enough, a referee can indeed undo your chances of landing that dream job. So how should you think of choosing and using a referee for a job application? Let's use the same principles marketers think of when using a celebrity to endorse their brands.

First, use referees who can help build your 'brand' the way you want to be positioned. Don't just choose people because you've worked with them or because of their designation. Every job and every role has certain specific skills and fit areas which are more critical than others. You need to be aware of what those are, and be clear on how you are differentiated on those by way of your experiences and accomplishments. That's why if you are indeed applying for jobs and have a couple of interviews lined up, don't just blindly offer up the same list of referees. Be clear on what each job involves and what you bring to the party for each that could set you apart. Then choose referees who could strengthen and add credibility to those points of difference.

It may sound simple enough, but it does require conscious thought. I've had personal examples where people have reached out to me for references. When I read further, they were applying for a senior-level job where a critical skill area called for managing large and dispersed teams. The problem was that I had managed them when they were very junior in their careers and had no people management experience. So while I could vouch for them as individual contributors, I could really say nothing about how they would be as managers. So don't just pick a referee because you worked for them, but pick one who can endorse the specific skill sets you want to highlight. Next, once you have chosen your referee, don't just put their name on your list and drop them a mail or call to ask them. Have a deliberate conversation regarding the job you're applying for and discuss the key experiences and skills needed. Play up areas you'd like to highlight from the time you worked together. No, there's nothing wrong in doing that. In one shot, you end up reminding them of the work you've done (don't flatter yourself with the thought that every manager will remember every single project you did) and also reinforce key talking points. This also brings up a common folly—simply picking past bosses or managers you know with fancy designations. This is the equivalent of defaulting to a Bollywood starlet. If a role calls for managing a matrix organization or working with multifunctional peers a lot, in addition to your past managers it may be good to serve up peers who've worked with you in similar situations. If it's building a team that counts, offer up those who have reported to you in the past and can vouch for your ability to build and motivate a team.

Next comes the question of credibility. Indeed in this case it could be a mismatch between what you hope your referee says and what he or she actually ends up saying. Such a discrepancy can be an instant killer of any opportunity you may be pursuing.

What happens when you use the old boss as a referee is the very real possibility that the boss ends up saying something that, far from helping your cause, actually hurts it. It may sound a simple enough mistake to avoid, but too many people end up giving their former bosses or managers as referees. They do this independent of how their performance in that role was and how that particular manager viewed them. People assume that the manager in question will sing their praises even if their performance in that particular role was below par. The bottom line is that just as you are trying to build your 'equity' as a candidate, your referees have equities and reputations of their own. When asked for a reference or background check, they will not say things which are untruthful. Just as a celebrity will not endorse a product they may not believe in, a referee will not say you're the best thing since sliced bread if their experience with you has been lukewarm. Of course, they'll be polite and professional, but an experienced headhunter or hiring manager knows when a referee is genuinely endorsing someone and when not. If they simply decline to provide a reference, that in itself sends a clear signal to a hiring firm or a headhunter. Also, you need to factor in the fact that if you're choosing a senior referee, there is the real possibility that the headhunter knows him or her (and in this day and age of LinkedIn, the chances are pretty good they're 'connected'). So the referee gains nothing by hurting their own credibility and giving an overly generous reference if they do not really believe in it. The onus is of course on you. Hence pick referees who don't just have a big designation, but whom you know will have a favourable opinion of you. Your referee should personally vouch for you. If you've worked for many managers, ask yourself whom you had the best performance working for. And that works on multiple levels—your referee also has a CV and for that particular role, you looking good makes them also look good.

Finally, choose referees who are on the upswing, or at least not going through major change or transitions of their own. Yes, you can never predict if a referee will go the way of Tiger Woods or Lance Armstrong, and those are extreme examples. But you can do your homework. If the referee you're thinking of has just changed jobs or is between jobs, spare a thought for them and their careers. That may not be the best time to ask them for a recommendation since it's likely that they are talking to headhunters about their own careers, and may not really engage to the extent you'd want them to. Also, do your homework on what happened to a business and a team you were on after you left. Especially at senior levels, headhunters and hiring managers want to know not just that you can deliver while you're on the job but that you can create sustained results. If you had a good run, but the business collapsed soon thereafter, chances are your boss at that time wasn't too happy and probably didn't come out smelling of roses.

If you have to take an overall thought away, let it be that if you're a brand then these referees are just the endorsers. A fancy list of referees will not make up for you not pitching yourself appropriately and what you bring to the table. Combining a couple of analogies we've used so far, the box of detergent which shows up with the claim 'cleans clothes' will likely not sell too much even if a hot new Bollywood starlet holds it up and flashes her brightest smile.

So far we've talked about many of the common things a marketer needs to do—position a brand, get trial, get loyalty and build credibility for the brand among its consumers. We have talked a lot about what marketers have learned it takes to succeed in each of these tasks, but now we'll shift gears a bit, and discuss something that every marketer must also face in the course of their careers.

Failure.

•••

THE THREE MANTRAS OF THE SHASTRA OF SEEKING ENDORSEMENT

- When it comes to referees or endorsers, one size does not fit all. Be deliberate in what you are seeking an endorsement on (whether it be for a job or a marriage proposal), and choose a referee who will strengthen your 'equity' for that opportunity, not just someone senior or with a fancy designation.

- The big killer in any endorsement is when the claim does not match the actual belief of the endorser in the brand (in this case, you!). So do your homework and groundwork on choosing referees who will not just speak positively of you, but on the specific aspects you want to get endorsement on.

- Spare a thought for the endorser. They are human beings as well. Be sensitive to them, to the fact that they are endorsing you as a priority in spite of other changes or crises in their lives. That's why it is perhaps best to maintain relationships with people instead of popping up in their inboxes out of the blue asking for an endorsement.

The Shastra of Dealing with Failure

Lessons for Bouncing Back in Style

To a layperson, marketing often seems glamorous and exciting because it involves so much visible innovation and creativity. There are new products being launched, new business ideas being brought to market and new ads proclaiming the benefits of these products and ideas in as appealing a manner as possible. All of that glitz and glamour is very prominent, and anyone who watches television or surfs the net cannot help but notice them. It makes for great dinnertime conversation when a marketer is asked whether they got to meet the celebrity at an ad shoot. I am sure it's a good feeling when they are asked when the next cool product is coming into the marketplace. What is not so visible, and sometimes remains a secret known only to those who spend many years in the field of marketing, is a simple unglamorous truth.

Failure is part and parcel of being a marketer. For every time a marketer scores a success, there will be another time when they fail.

There are all kinds of studies out there on the success rate of new product launches, and to be honest, some of them go as far as to say that more than 90 per cent of them fail. Many of them may be overstating their results because of how 'success' is defined, sometimes a very short-term measure like first-year sales. What I have seen in my experience is perhaps closer to what a study done in the United States by the Product Development and Management Association in 2004 showed. According to the study, depending on the sector, failure rates (defined as the inability to meet commercial objectives set out by the organization before launch) were in the forties, with fast-moving consumer goods (FMCG) at 49 per cent.

Think about it. All the money well-known companies and their marketers spend on research and planning, and you could flip a coin and decide whether to launch that next new product or not, since the odds of success are actually not much better than calling heads or tails on tossing a coin. That's because marketing is hardly an exact science. It's fundamentally not about models or theories, but about human behaviour. We all know how fickle and unpredictable that can be. Tastes change, habits change, new brands come into the market to change the competitive set-up you're up against and what in pre-market research seemed a great idea fails when launched in the market. For marketers, this failure can be intensely personal. You could have spent months, or even years, of your life working on a new idea or business. When that fails, it's not just something you write a report about and move on with the job. That rejection, and that is what it is, a rejection by the consumer and the market, is something that really strikes home hard.

Being a marketer and building a career in marketing means that you have to learn not just to deal with failure and rejection, but indeed take it in your stride and also bounce back. How do marketers do that?

First, when they fail, marketers don't just fret and agonize (well, they do that, but then they also move on), they try and figure out what happened. When people think of market research, they usually focus on all the testing that happens *before* a product or idea is launched. However, the reality is that a lot of research and analysis goes into understanding what happened when or *after* that idea or product was launched. This serves two important purposes for a marketer. For one, to get early learning so that course corrections can be made and a launch that is off-track can be brought back in line. And second, even if that particular launch fails, new learning is fostered so that chances of future success are increased. Typically, this will take the form of a systematic tracking after an idea is put into the market, measuring various inputs and outputs. On the input side, a marketer may measure spending levels, supply availability, pricing etc. On the output side, the measures will include things like awareness, trial, distribution, market share, average spending per customer and so on. These measures help a marketer understand whether a launch is off-track because:

- The plans that were made before the launch were not delivered. One of the most common reasons for failure is that spending was not sustained at the levels that were assumed, either because the company had profit pressures or other priorities to fund. A study by research giant Nielsen in 2011 showed that in India, given the trade environment of largely smaller stores where distribution may take time to build up, new launches often need months to really take off. Hence they also need sustained investment and effort over that gestation period. Impulse categories like food could reach their 'inflection point' (when the idea or product really reaches a critical mass that can be considered sustainable success) within months but categories where there is more loyalty, like personal care, could take up to two years. Often where ideas fail is that marketers don't have the patience or discipline to hang in there and give up too early, such that the investment levels that were built into projections never get delivered in the real world.

• The plans were delivered but the launch still failed because something happened in the external environment, for example actions by competitors or consumer preference changes. A classic recent case is the Indian mobile phone market. Nokia had historically dominated this space and continued with its game plan that had worked for it for years and led it to market leadership. What changed was not its own planning or the launches and campaigns it had in the pipeline, but the fact that the competitive space transformed with Samsung emerging as a strong contender and with consumer preference starting to shift decisively towards Samsung and the Android Operating System it had. In just one year, between 2011–12 and 2012–13, Nokia's market share fell by more than ten points, from close to 38 per cent to 27 per cent, while Samsung gained market leadership. The models launched by Nokia in this period all failed to meet their objectives, not because there was anything inherently different in how they were launched compared to their previous plans or how they were conceived, but because the external and competitive environment had changed and Nokia had not anticipated or planned for it. [1]

In either scenario, a good marketer will compile learning early and adjust plans accordingly. If the inputs are not on track as to what was needed to succeed, then the organization needs to decide whether to keep investing in the idea, or if required, spend somewhere else. On the other hand, if competition has done something to disrupt the planned launch or consumer preferences have changed, then the company needs to respond appropriately. Either way, the focus is on action-based reflection and analysis to either turn around a failure, or indeed increase chances of future success.

The second thing most marketers do to learn early and maximize their chances of future success is to initiate into test markets, learning markets and so on, often referred to by different names in different companies. But whatever the name used, the principle is the same: try out your idea in a smaller market or group of consumers. Even better, try out multiple small pilots at the same time so you can understand what works and what doesn't, and refine your plans before you really spend the big bucks. For the most successful marketers, this takes the form of iterative learning, where ideas and stimuli (packaging, product, communication etc.) are put in front of consumers throughout the development process. Dr Robert Cooper, one of the foremost authorities on new product successes, and author of the bestselling *Winning at New Products* calls this way of working 'spiral development'. In his words, instead of developing everything and then throwing it out there, the companies that are best at new product success, ' . . . build in a series of iterative steps, or loops, whereby successive versions of the product are shown to the customer to seek feedback and verification'. What this means is that they keep trying out variations of ideas to see how they can improve and better meet consumer needs, and it is through this process that they get winning solutions, versus putting out one 'perfect' version that either works or fails.

Dr Cooper should know. Over forty years of his career, he has studied more than 3000 new product successes and failures. He found that when you separated out successful innovators from those who fail, you would find that among the successful ones, the percentage of those who followed such a learning and development process was six times higher than among the failures. Sometimes, marketers get the kind of learning through such an exercise that they build into a broader launch, and sometimes, they conclude that the idea is best abandoned. But then that decision is taken before a lot of time, energy and yes, funds have been spent on launching it and then failing on a much larger scale. The best marketers don't just do this kind of learning to increase chances of success, but also to keep pushing the envelope and to see how far they can go with their innovation. Far from managing risk of failure, this becomes a way to keep on learning and can sometimes generate new, big ideas that turn what may have looked like failure into something much bigger. In the early 2000s, Procter & Gamble began test marketing PUR, a brand of water purification, which promised to revolutionize how poor consumers in developing markets could get safe drinking water. The product was a powder that when simply stirred into water and then strained would decontaminate water and make it fit for drinking. The test markets did not work, and it may have been easy to give up on the idea. While the commercial model did not work to the company's expectations, the potential of the product in improving health and producing safer drinking water was apparent. The 2004 tsunami in the Indian Ocean was a pivotal moment, when P&G donated 13 million packets of PUR to affected people in Sri Lanka, the Maldives and Indonesia. The impact PUR had on saving lives and helping people in times of crisis when safe drinking water was a critical need led to a huge corporate social responsibility effort that is called Children's Safe Drinking Water. Working with the Clinton Global Initiative, a force for positive change started by President Bill Clinton, this quickly expanded as a way to provide safe drinking water to needy people worldwide. It was voted as one of the world's most amazing social innovations by the *Economist* in 2012 and turned a commercial test-market failure into something that has earned P&G immense goodwill.

And it has made a real difference. By 2013, this effort had helped save an estimated 32,000 lives across seventy-one markets. Now, that is truly an example of how an idea that failed led to insights that created a huge impact.

• • •

Dealing with failure and learning how to bounce back from it is of course something we all deal with, because while we all plan for success and happiness, we all know that along the way, we will have to face our share of disappointments as well. Depending on your stage of life, you can think of occasions relevant to you where something you have planned and hoped for hasn't quite worked out. I would venture a guess that heartbreak, or being turned down by someone we liked, would perhaps be on that list for many of us. Perhaps not getting into an educational course or job we had applied for and really wanted would be another. Or for the parents among you, sometimes just as you experience success through your kids, you also experience their disappointment, for example when a much-coveted and practised-for place on a sports team or in the school play doesn't work out. All of these occasions have something in common, which is the disappointment that comes with failing in something you had really prepared for and invested emotionally in. In dealing with many of these instances, the principles I've mentioned above in this chapter can help. Think about it—many of us have at one point or the other, had a failed relationship. The advice, whether from well-meaning friends, or from self-help gurus, is consistent:

- Don't give up. The worst thing to do is to lose faith in relationships because of one bad experience. As the cliché goes, there are plenty of fish out there in the sea.
- Don't blame yourself or the other person blindly but try and understand what went wrong so you avoid the same mistakes in future.
- Get yourself out there again. Meet new people, make friends.

Sound familiar? All very similar in principle to what marketers do to rebound from failed initiatives.

Before we move to one particular application in our daily lives of how marketing thinking can help in bouncing back from such failure, let me share a story about myself. My first novel was a coming-of-age novel called *The Funda of Mix-ology*, a story about a young man coming to grips with pursuing his career in the corporate sector while trying not to totally abandon his dream of being a writer. As you may guess, it was written straight from the heart and I had vested a lot of my emotions into this book. When it actually came to getting it out to readers, I was a complete novice. I had no idea how the world of publishing worked. With all the confidence and zeal of someone in his twenties and the labour of his love to share with the world, I sent out the manuscript with submission letters to dozens of publishers in India and around the world. The crushing disappointment I got was perhaps worse than most marketers would face on a product launch. I received fifty-four rejection letters. Yes, fifty-four. From all around the world, a stack of letters that if stapled together would look like a pretty good-sized book in its own right. Of course I spent my share of time moping and venting about the injustice of it all, but then I put my energies to getting this failed 'launch' back on track.

To bounce back, I did the two things I mentioned before:

• I really tried to understand where I had gone wrong. In trying to be relevant to everyone, I wasn't being relevant to anyone. My novel was set in an unnamed city, and the characters had generic names. I rewrote it to be sharply positioned in Mumbai and brought in a lot more of the Indian context of pressures to do well in one's career and of dreams postponed due to the rat race.

• I did my own version of test marketing. While I refined my novel, I got my writing 'out there' in front of readers through a weekly column on sify.com. The positive reactions of readers certainly helped feed my confidence and also helped me refine my ideas and craft.

I also did my own research into how the book publishing business worked, and the first realization was that it was a business! I had been naive enough to send out my novel, believing that all that mattered was the creative idea. However, like any other business, a publishing house has to see the commercial prospect of a novel which stems from the target it is pitched at, how it is differentiated from other books in the genre and the likely appeal. These questions are not very different from what marketers face. As I took a breather to introspect and improve, the novel became much more sharply focused. It built off topical issues in India and yes, with the added practice I got, I did become a better writer.

When *The Funda of Mix-ology* was finally picked up by a publishing house in India, it went on to become a national bestseller and marked the real inflection point of my writing career. The initial visibility and reviews it got certainly built up my confidence to work on the next novel, and when I was ready with it, I had learned much more about the publishing world and could approach things differently. Instead of sending out the manuscript to all and sundry, I got help from a wonderful pair of agents, and my next novel, *Herogiri*, was published by Random House. One thing led to another, and soon I was personally connected with editors at major publishers so that I could bounce ideas off them. I could send my initial work to them directly and then focus on my writing instead of dreading another mountain of rejection slips.

Sometimes people ask if it was the initial success that led to more novels and deals, which was the turning point. I say that the real turning point was the rejections I received, which forced me to introspect, learn and improve.

• • •

We all plan to succeed, but need to learn to deal with failure, and we will apply this learning to try and answer a question which would have an impact on millions of ordinary Indians, not just marketers at multinational firms.

How could we take this learning to improve the chances of success of our own entrepreneurial ventures? In recent years, there has been a lot of attention and coverage focused on the emerging 'start-up culture' in India and certainly, start-ups are growing at a rapid pace. In late 2014, the National Association of Software and Services Companies (NASSCOM) estimated that India already had the world's third largest start-up ecosystem after the United States and the United Kingdom, with approximately 3100 in existence and more than 800 being set up each year. You perhaps personally know of some young, bright kid in the family who after completing an engineering or business degree, instead of taking up a job, decided to start up on their own. One mistake would be to ascribe this trend entirely to IIT whiz-kids or the Internet start-up boom. The reality is that India is a nation of entrepreneurs. *Inc.* magazine is one of the premier publications for entrepreneurs and business owners. In a January 2015 article titled, 'Why India is the Land of Rising Entrepreneurship', it touched upon entrepreneurs in India and the challenges they faced. According to the article, in 2014 it was estimated that India had 48 million entrepreneurs, more than double that of the United States (at 23 million). The owners of these 'Micro, Small and Medium enterprises', as the government classifies them, play a critical role in making our nation run. They account for 45 per cent of manufacturing output, 40 per cent of exports and are the biggest employment generators after agriculture. Ranging from the neighbourhood grocery store set up by a housewife (40 per cent of entrepreneurial ventures in India are in fact retail) to a website set up by IIT grads, the failure rate of these ventures is staggeringly high. While the specific number being quoted differs, the World Economic Forum in late 2014 mentioned a failure rate of 90 per cent. That is in line with the failure rate quoted by *Fortune* magazine on a feature on start-ups in September 2014.

Think about it. A 90 per cent failure rate means that nine of ten new ventures will fail. We talked about the pressures marketers feel with a failure rate of one in two. But in their case, they are doing jobs. While a failed major launch may result in poor performance reviews and a lot of disappointment, they can always look for another chance, or in the worst case change their jobs and start afresh. For an entrepreneur, the stakes are very different. It's their own savings, livelihood and dreams at stake, and nine out of ten times, they will fail. My intent is not to spook any potential or young entrepreneur, since clearly Indians have the entrepreneurial spirit well entrenched in them. I am only interested to see how we could apply the lessons learned by consumer marketers over decades of experience to improve an entrepreneur's chances of success. A 'failure rate' of nine in ten need not be the end of the story. What will matter is how many of them can bounce back and turn early setbacks into lasting successes.

And such learning may be much needed in India. Research conducted by Gallup in 2012 showed that only 22 per cent of entrepreneurs in India who wanted to start their business in the next twelve months had any formal training or exposure to running a business—that is, half the Asian average of 44 per cent. Part of setting your venture up for success is to ensure your offering meets a need, is differentiated versus what else is out there, and that you have a real plan to build trial and loyalty. While hardly a comprehensive education on the subject, the preceding chapters may help anyone starting out on their own think through how they could create a business model that may increase chances of success, which in itself is half the battle won.

In a late 2014 interview in the *Economic Times*, Rahul Sood, a serial Silicon Valley entrepreneur and head of the entrepreneurship acceleration arm at Microsoft, had a harsh but simple answer to the failure rate and weaknesses of start-ups in India: 'Mostly half-baked, with no customer validation'. Understanding the consumer idea and the strategy to differentiate and build trial and loyalty would be a missing link most entrepreneurs would do well to embrace to further increase their chances of success. But so do consumer marketers, and they still fail. So how could an entrepreneur apply the principles we've covered in this chapter?

First, you need to acknowledge the fact that the chances of initial failure or setbacks are very high. Too many people read about the start-up boom and start thinking that it's just a matter of creating a site and getting some funding and they're on their way to becoming the next Flipkart. That's the thing with bubbles—people look at the examples of extreme success and ignore the statistical probability of failure. The early setbacks often result in disheartening them even more and they give up. Perhaps hanging in there with a bit more discipline may well have turned things around. So realizing that instant success is not guaranteed, or even likely, is important to have as a part of the mindset. This leads to more strategic preparation, such as having some savings set aside, say, to pay the bills while the new venture gets off the ground, thereby setting more realistic goals so that you don't give up too early and so on.

Next is to be clear on what you think will lead to the results you want and then track them. If you're opening a neighbourhood bakery, how many people a day do you anticipate will walk in the door, and how much on average will they spend per bill? What are your assumptions on food and other costs? Then, when you begin, do what professional marketers do. Keep tracking and understanding how you are doing on those assumptions. That way you don't just look at one overall number of revenue or profit, but you are able to understand what factors are driving those numbers as well. You don't need much by way of statistical training or analysis, just an Excel sheet and a clear understanding of what is meant to get you your desired business results. If you're not getting enough people through the door (or clicking on your site, as the case may be), then you can double-click on that issue and determine whether it's because not enough people are aware of your business or that they are aware but not preferring you. Each of these identifications will have its own specific fixes—creating awareness or driving a more differentiated message or positioning respectively. Six chapters in, I hope you are starting to see that marketing really isn't rocket science, and indeed, I firmly believe you don't need an MBA to do it. You just need to be clear on the behaviour you want to drive among your consumers and you need to know the right questions to ask. Given the lack of business training or education among most entrepreneurs in India, the battle is sometimes lost even before it is fought. This is because just seeing sales and profit numbers by themselves rarely offer up insights or ideas to turn around a failure. What is needed is digging beyond the numbers to understand root causes and possible fixes. These could stem from either wrong strategic choices on what to offer the consumer or operating issues in actually delivering to the consumer what is promised. Even among funded and well-staffed start-ups, the focus initially tends to be funding and technology, not the consumer and on understanding the 'why' behind consumer behaviour. So if you're starting up a business, or know someone who is, get an Excel sheet open, force yourself to put those assumptions down, track them and then act on what you find. You will be channelling the combined experiences of thousands of professional marketers who have been doing the same for years on end and could well find yourself on the right side of the 90:10 equation when it comes to successful new ventures.

The final leaf to take out of the playbook of professional marketers is to keep learning and iterating. Many start-ups by definition do learning, or beta-testing, or start small before scaling up.

So testing is something most entrepreneurs do, sometimes simply because demonstrating early success is important to attract funding, or to build confidence in themselves to invest more in the venture. What many entrepreneurs do not do is ironically what professional marketers do often, which is consciously to test different executions to see which one has the best results before scaling up. So if you are running a neighbourhood bakery, try out different menus in different weeks, try out different signage to see which one attracts people more or determine whether putting a flyer in the neighbourhood newspaper brings in any more visitors than without it. Within a month or so, it will be possible to get clear and actionable learning on which elements of your plan work and also what they may be impacting. Marketers also test 'how high is high'—when a planned element works, how do you know you are doing enough of it? Assume that the flyer you sent out attracted many more visitors to your bakery, would you get even more if you ran it twice a month? If you run a service that runs off an app, if offering a discount of 10 per cent on a service got you a certain number of orders, should you test what a 20 per cent discount does?

Learning to rebound from early setbacks is what makes the difference between successful marketers and those who throw in the towel at the first sign of failure, and that is what could also make the difference for you if you're thinking of starting up on your own.

•••

THE THREE MANTRAS OF THE SHASTRA OF DEALING WITH FAILURE

- Instead of expecting success as an entitlement, realize that failure is part and parcel of the journey. Preparing only for success can lead to disappointment and giving up at the first sign of adversity—whether it is a relationship, business or venture. Indeed, the ideas, relationships and ventures that endure are often those that have weathered storms of failure.

- Don't just focus on the outcome (the 'what')—whether it's financial measures, a rejected manuscript or a proposal that's turned down. Also look at the 'why'—the underlying reasons. That will give insights and ideas on how you can bounce back in the future.

- Keep learning and trying out new ways to succeed. Curiosity is your best friend when trying something new, and complacency your worst enemy. Try out new ideas, learn what works and what doesn't, instead of assuming success is getting one 'right' answer the first time around.

8
The Shastra of Optimizing Marketing Spending

Lessons in Managing the ROI of Office Hours

DAD, DON'T YOU THINK THE ROI OF GIVING ME THE ICE CREAM IS HIGHER THAN ME COMING TO YOU EVERY FIVE MINUTES ASKING YOU FOR IT?

BRAND SHASTRA

To someone who's not in the industry, it may look like marketers have unlimited budgets. Surely all that advertising on television, those front-page print ads and indeed, the amounts the Bollywood celebrities charge for using their carefully made-up faces to endorse brands must add up to a hefty amount? And it certainly does. In 2015, according to media agency GroupM, total advertising expenditure in India was estimated to be close to Rs 50,000 crore, up 12.6 per cent compared to the previous year. While on the one hand that sounds like a lot of money, the reality is also that no marketing manager will ever tell you that he or she has unlimited budgets. Part of that is human psychology—when is the last time we said we were paid enough or had enough resources or budgets? But part of that is the reality that, especially given the current economic uncertainty and the fast pace at which consumers and media are evolving, marketers in all industries are being asked one question: Are we sure we're spending enough, and not too much?

Quickly followed by another question: Are we sure we're spending on the right things?

In answering those questions, modern marketers channel the thoughts and frustrations of a fascinating man who lived close to a century ago. John Wanamaker was a merchant, political leader and philanthropist who lived in the United States between 1838 and 1922. In some ways, he was a visionary—while he did not invent the fixed price system, he was the first to use price tags on goods in his stores. He was a true trailblazer when it came to using advertising to build business, being the first retailer to place a half-page print ad and the first full-page print ad in 1879. He is also widely credited as being one of the pioneers in using mass media. He was a visionary when it came to treating his employees well, providing recreational facilities, free medical care and profit-sharing plans long before these were considered industry standard. Pity they did not have social media back then, or awards for the best places to work, else he would have topped those lists. The facilities at his workplace would have been getting the same kind of rave reviews the way, say, a Google office gets today. He also made notable efforts to provide more equal opportunities to African Americans and Native Americans.

But Wanamaker may not have had the same insight outside the world of business. In 1893, as the then United States postmaster general, he proclaimed at the Chicago World Fair that the US postal system would rely on horses and stagecoaches for a century to come, as automobiles would remain a passing fad. Be that as it may, he made a lasting impact on the world of marketing. Many marketers today seek to answer a question he raised, without perhaps even realizing that it was John Wanamaker who made this famous statement: 'Half the money I spend on advertising is wasted. The trouble is I don't know which half.'

Today, marketers spend a lot of time and effort trying to understand the right way to spend their marketing money, and one of the tools they use is called Return on Investment, or ROI. ROI is simply a way to examine how much return each rupee spent on a particular element of the marketing mix brings in as revenue. By doing this, a marketer could try and optimize overall spending.

As an example, let's say a marketer is spending Rs 1000 on TV advertising and Rs 250 on digital. Through tools like 'Market Mix Modelling', this marketer may learn that they are spending more than is needed on TV and not enough on digital and reallocate spending to get more growth within the same budget. We will not delve into the technicalities of how such tools are used, but let's explore the principles and thought processes marketers use to answer such questions and find the best ROI their marketing budgets can deliver.

The first is not to take any part of the marketing budget as a 'given' but to put it all up for question and reallocation. What often happens is that some spending occurs on 'autopilot', essentially the team saying, 'we spent x per cent on promotions last year, so we'll assume we'll do the same this year.' The basic principle of using ROI is not to do that but to open up all spending to question. In the industry, that's sometimes called 'zero based budgeting' and what it means in simple English is that if you assume that you were starting your business from scratch, how would you spend your money? Quite often, the first savings are found when teams challenge activities or plans which are being spent against purely because that is the way things have been done in the past.

At a macro level, the media expenditure for India quoted above shows such choices being made. While overall spending was up 12.6 per cent in 2015, digital spending is up 37 per cent while spending on magazines is actually down 4 per cent.[1] At an aggregate level, marketers are questioning where they spend their money as consumer habits change and instead of spending a certain amount on magazines because they always have, they are tailoring their spend levels and spending more on a medium where consumers are clearly spending more time and attention—on the Internet.

In answering Wanamaker's immortal question, the first step many marketers take is truly to put their entire spend bucket on the table and consider it in totality. Otherwise, the risk of taking something 'for granted' is that while you may have spent on a particular item in the past, the environment, media habits or consumer preferences may have changed and not questioning that may mean not touching one or more elements of your marketing plan that truly are not working for you anymore. More than just the business and numbers, what using the concept of ROI does is to get marketers into a mindset of constantly evaluating choices and not having any 'holy cows'. Everything is up for question and there is an unstated acceptance of the fact that things do change, and we must be open and agile enough to embrace those changes. That's what the best marketers do, and in doing so, they don't wait for their media rupees to stop working or for a fancy 'Market Mix Modelling' presentation, but they know what the trends are, and they proactively question choices and adjust and improve.

The second thing a marketer does when using the concept of ROI is to be clear on what success looks like— efficiency or effectiveness? Sometimes a company or a sector as a whole may be focused on creating explosive growth and not generating short-term profitability. Success is measured not by how efficiently the money is spent, but on the absolute impact it has and how fast it can help scale up the business. A classic example from recent times would be the e-commerce sector in India. In 2014, the three big players—Flipkart, Amazon and Snapdeal—had combined net revenues of Rs 3200 crore. In the same period, they spent almost Rs 500 crore on advertising alone, not including what they would have paid for celebrity endorsements, production costs and event sponsorships. And that's not even counting all the money they would be spending on the discounting and promotions they run, which would be considered promotional spending in many industries. That is a lot of money to be spending on marketing in total, and while the total pool of spending they are doing on a growing scale is not available in the public domain, we get the idea of just how disproportionate their spending is. The net loss of these three companies for the same period was a whopping Rs 985 crore, as per filings with the Registrar of Companies.[2]

All these numbers mean that for every rupee of sale, they are losing close to thirty paise, but that is not necessarily something that bothers them. Since these are early years of their growth, short-term profit may not be their biggest consideration. Their marketing teams are focused on rapidly scaling up brand awareness and revenue, both to get larger sales and consumer bases faster and also to continue attracting investments, since their spending is fuelled by private equity (and global war chests, in the case of Amazon). It may make sense for them given the context they are operating in, but for a more traditional business (a long-standing public listed company in a stable industry, for example) this would be heresy. This is because the circumstances are different. A public-listed company is responsible to deliver predictable returns to shareholders as compared to a funded company which has the deep pockets of PE firms to dip into.

When the cash profits you generate are what fund your marketing, and indeed your ability to pay employees' salaries, you are likely to take a much deeper look at where you're spending your marketing money. Let's take the team at Hindustan Unilever, for example—a large firm which is publicly listed and has to fund its own growth and provide steady returns to shareholders. While the marketers will focus on growth, their ideas and proposals will always be vetted by their finance counterparts and bosses to see whether they make the right short-term financial returns and generate the desired ROI. Sometimes a publicly listed firm will also bet for the long-term, and choose not to make money on an idea for the short-term, but it will manage its portfolio to ensure that it can still deliver short-term results.

Also, the question of what is a priority, efficiency or effectiveness, is something that needs to be revisited and can change over time. Even for e-commerce firms like Amazon and Flipkart, the question is rapidly shifting to one of what a sustainable business model looks like. Increasingly marketers and leaders at these firms are looking at how they can strike a better balance between growth and profitability. As a couple of recent examples, housing.com is not likely to go and spend Rs 120 crore on a Rs 2 crore revenue base again in a hurry after all, especially given the scrutiny and management changes that came before. Among the more established e-commerce firms, many are reportedly soul-searching about finding a more sustainable business model.[3]

Once you're clear on the objective of the marketing plan (efficiency or effectiveness), a marketer then goes into action using something called 'cascading choices'. The concept of cascading choices says that you should rank in descending order of importance the choices you have, and then work your way down the list. You move to the next item only when you are satisfied that you have done all you can with the more important item. In the all-too-familiar situation of making spending choices with limited and often shrinking marketing budgets, this is a great way to force yourself to prioritize the most important elements of your marketing strategy. This way you can avoid spreading money thinly all around, which in my experience is not the ideal way.

In a marketing context, you would need to start with an understanding of the various media you could use, and some insight into their relative importance for your brand or category. You may or may not have access to tools that can quantify this, but if nothing else, your judgement, past experience and competitive benchmarking can quickly yield this information. Suppose the list for your brand reads like this:

- TV
- In-store displays
- Online advertising
- Outdoor advertising
- Print

The next step is to determine what would be optimal spending levels on each of these media channels for your brand. Marketers determine this in a number of ways: What is needed to meet awareness and reach targets, the levels that have been proven to work in the past, the levels at which your key competitors are operating, and so on. Once you have this information, it's time to get cracking on 'cascading choices'.

If you were to follow the concept of cascading choices literally, you would take your marketing budget and allocate the optimum amount to the most important item (TV in this case), and then work your way down to the next item. You would repeat this process until you ran out of money or items to spend on. So what does 'cascading choices' offer? It forces us to be ruthlessly selective and decisive.

The final thought on ROI is that marketers need to understand where there may be 'spikes' or seasonality in their business. By doing so, they focus their spending around those particular times. A few examples could be New Year blowout sales for e-commerce or retail chains, Diwali for chocolate companies or Christmas for bakeries. Every business has some times of the year when consumption spikes and consumers enter the category in higher numbers or consume more than they normally would. Identifying and understanding these periods is critical because the ROI of every rupee spent on marketing is not equal throughout the year. If a marketer spends wisely through the year, but at a critical consumption period does not have sufficient spending, all that hard work could be undone. Such planning is especially critical because many of these 'spikes' are created by seasons, holidays or events which affect shopping behaviour for the entire category, not just one company. So if a brand does not anticipate when such spikes will occur and be ready to spend then, it could lose out in a big way to its competitors. A classic case for many marketers who advertise on television is the spike in rates and clutter caused by big cricket tournaments like the World Cup or the IPL. During the 2015 Cricket World Cup, ad rates were up almost 50 per cent versus the previous tournament. For a marketer who wants to target those watching the tournament or is planning a heavy ad blitz at this time, buying media time with the 'usual' budgets or definitions of ROI will likely mean very poor results.

• • •

You don't have to be managing marketing budgets to use many of these principles on a day-to-day basis. Any housewife who is trying to balance her budgets with the needs and wants of her family members intuitively knows what these marketers are trying to do—make every rupee stretch further and try and prioritize between what is nice to have and what is critical to have. They may not have fancy market mix modelling, but they know well what are the essentials (rent, food, education) and then what are the discretionary items (eating out, holidays) and also what are the 'spikes' where increased spending is necessary (birthdays, anniversaries). I still remember as a child my mother managing our home on what was the modest salary of a government servant. We were never left wanting, got the best education our parents could afford, yet were on occasions gently nudged away from what may have been extravagances ('we'll get you that toy you want on your birthday, not now'). My mother may never have done an MBA, but like so many mothers around India, she ran a tight ship that would have done any marketer proud. When I was in school, I remember a census-taker coming home and chatting with my mother about patterns of expenditure. I was amazed as I saw my mother rattle off how much was spent under different expense heads, and how much was saved each month, all without looking at a single number or piece of paper.

Managing within constraints and making the right choice on where to spend or use those constrained resources is something every single one of us does—not only on household budgets, but also at work where we have to decide how to allot people against tasks or targets, or indeed in our personal lives. I would argue the same thinking applies beyond just us and our daily lives. If I look at the arena of sports, for example cricket, a team is constantly making resource allocation decisions. How many bowlers to play? Which batsman to send in at what time given the tasks ahead? How to pace the innings to get the most runs out of a finite set of overs or chase a target given certain overs? In test matches, whether to declare or not? They all come back to the same core question that marketers deal with in making decisions on ROI and marketing spending. Given finite resources, how do you best use them to deliver the best results?

One of the areas where I try and consciously use this concept is in managing the various aspects of my life. Like you, dear reader, I have a family, and I want to do the best for them and be there for them. I also have a full-time job which can take up as much of my time and energy as I'm willing to expend on it. Then comes my writing, something I've been passionate about since I was a child and a practice I want truly to nurture and keep alive. Then there's also the want to keep some time for fitness and my own health. As you can see, the things I need to fit into my life already makes for a pretty long list. And that's not even including time for friends, social commitments, travel and so on. So fitting all of them in and, more importantly, doing justice to all of them is something that is important to me, and one area where I've found my experiences and learning in the world of business and marketing have actually helped a lot.

• • •

So, let's take some of this learning and apply it to a scenario so many of us encounter in our daily lives: one where we are looking at how best to spend a limited resource (and in this case, all of us have the same 'budget'—twenty-four hours a day) among competing areas we can spend our time on. Chances are most people are even more confused about this conundrum than Wanamaker was when he was deciding his marketing budget.

I'm talking about the issue of striking the right work–life balance.

In every workplace, and for everyone who has a family member who works a job, maintaining a work–life balance is a big challenge. It is often demanded but rarely achieved. The extent to which this matters can be gauged from the results of the NDTV survey on New Years' resolutions I mentioned in Chapter 4. After wanting to lose weight, the desire to get better work–life balance was the single-most important resolution among Indians, almost double that of the next highest one on the list. Thus, this is a very real problem, and I'm sure that you, or someone you know, will relate to the challenges of finding the right balance between our professional and personal lives. Even if you don't count the intangible benefits of having more time for family and

other pursuits outside of work, research increasingly shows
that working smarter has real health benefits. A study carried
out by the University College of London, and reported in the
Guardian in August 2015, covering data from over six lakh
men and women across three countries, has concluded that
working fifty-five or more hours per week increases the risk
of a stroke by 33 per cent.[4] Yes, working too much is not
just something that you gripe about, it can literally kill you.
What's in it for employers? A simple fact—that providing
better work–life balance is going to be increasingly important
to attract and retain good talent. The Global Career
Aspiration Survey, conducted by Right Management across
ten countries including India, showed that work–life balance
is the number one career aspiration for employees, with
45 per cent of employees ranking it as the most important
facet of a job.

Given that employees want it and employers will benefit
from it, one would assume that providing better work–life
balance would be a focus area for both. Ideally, there should
be a number of solutions that have been created and put into
place to help employees achieve a better balance between
their personal and professional lives. The unfortunate answer
is a simple no. The biggest reason for that, in my opinion, is
that people have got the definition of work–life balance all
wrong. To get the right definition, we need to tap into what
marketers have learned about ROI.

The conventional definition of work–life balance for
many people and indeed, for many corporations, to me in

itself is flawed. It pits work, which is just one aspect of life, against life. The latter includes all the other roles we play outside of work, into one convenient and pithy word. That in itself sets most people up for failure because instead of looking at balancing the totality of all roles we play, it makes it seem all too simple. By definition the work–life dichotomy weighs the odds in favour of work because it takes work as almost a given, and everything else needs to be adjusted around it. That is the marketing equivalent of saying, 'let's take our TV budget aside since that is what it is, and then see how we can manage the rest of our budget and see how we can fit them all in.' Just as a marketer looks at zero based budgeting in determining ROI, you need to put work in its right perspective and place.

The first step is to recognize all the roles you play and all the stakeholders who count on you—at work and outside it. The starting point is to recognize that while what we do at work is an important part of our lives, it is by no means something that can be held as equally important or balanced against all the other roles we play—for our spouses, for our children, for our friends, for our own health, for our own passions and self-development, and indeed, for the community we live in.

It is crucial to realize that the true balance lies in doing full justice to all these roles, not in sacrificing one for the other. For me, that means being 100 per cent focused on work when I'm at work, but then when I'm with family or attending to my other responsibilities, to have the awareness and discipline not to let work intrude there. Just as it would be inappropriate for me to FaceTime my son in the middle of an office meeting, it is inappropriate for me to be responding to an office email when my son expects me to watch a movie with him. Awareness of the roles you play means little unless you have the discipline to know when you need to do justice to each of them. In this context, multitasking is a much abused word. My personal belief is that multitasking makes sense over time, in the sense that you will have a richer and more balanced life when you can ensure enough time and energy for all the things in your life. However, at any given point in time, it pays to be focused on what you're doing. So having a day where you're 'full on' at work and then spend time at the gym and have quality time with family is a good example of multitasking. Checking office email at the dining table and ignoring your child is a bad example of multitasking.

Also, just as a marketer watches for spikes or seasonality when normal definitions of ROI may not be appropriate, you need to be aware of 'spikes' in each aspect of your own life. The reality is that we will have emergencies at work and home, things that need to be done, times when people are really counting on us, etc. Where I've seen people get themselves into a negative spiral is when they ignore or are blind to these 'spikes', especially in aspects of their lives outside of work. An example of this is being with your kids when they have a function at school or a medical appointment, or indeed an anniversary or a birthday. A lot of people actually relish being the martyr and wearing as a badge of honour the fact that they missed these occasions due to work, perhaps in the mistaken belief that this will be seen as demonstrating more commitment to work. Then please don't complain about lack of balance! Just as you can be transparent with your family when something urgent needs to be done at work and you'll be held up late at office or will need to be away on a business trip for a long time, you should feel just as confident enough to tell your stakeholders at work when you need to take time off for the other aspects of life—and there are many, not just one big lumpy thing called 'life' to be balanced off against work. One of the simple tools I've found that can help in doing this is to 'integrate' work and personal calendars. A lot of people have their task lists and calendars for work, usually full of meetings and deadlines. They then have separate lists of things to do in their personal lives (reminders to pay bills, doctors' appointments etc.). Just try putting them together in one calendar, maybe by populating your personal reminders and tasks in your office calendar, and you may be surprised at the big difference such a small step makes. In one stroke, you get the 'full picture' of things you need to manage, and can then plan all your priorities accordingly, not try and finish everything for work at work and somehow figure out how to fit in other priorities.

Finally, remember that the definition of success will change over time. Just as a marketer may be focused on short-term profitability one year and long-term investment another, your life stages will change and priorities will change. What was an appropriate balance for me when I was a single employee in my early twenties changed when I got married, and then again when our son was born. Awareness of how your life is changing, with changing commitments and responsibilities, is in itself an important contributor to managing the right balance. The husband who keeps working late nights despite now having a family waiting for him at home has not taken into account his changed priorities, and put all of those into his own 'mix optimization'. To look at it from an organization's standpoint, the HR manager or boss who wonders why an employee is going home earlier than usual should perhaps be sensitive to what's happening in his or her life—a sickness in the family, for example, that could have changed priorities.

Remember also that work as you define it will change, and perhaps one day disappear from your life. On the other hand, many other aspects of life will not. As important as that meeting with the boss next week seems, one day your boss will change, your job will change, and indeed one day you won't have that designation or employee number to define you, no matter how important they seem today. But your family will still be there, your body and health will still be there, and if you're lucky, your dreams of all the things you wished you'd do if only you had 'more time' will be there. Don't wait for that day to realize that there was a lot more to life than some corporate platitudes about 'work–life balance'. And don't wait for that time to remember Wanamaker and think 'half the things I did with my life were wasted. The trouble is, I don't know which half'.

• • •

THE THREE MANTRAS OF THE SHASTRA OF FINDING AN OPTIMAL BALANCE

- Be conscious of all the things you need to balance and put them all out there ('zero based budgeting'— or if you're talking day-to-day work–life balance, the integrated calendar I mentioned). If you don't do that, it could lead to blind spots you end up ignoring.
- Be disciplined in following through on the choices you make. Whether it is a budget or the hours of the day to be balanced among competing priorities, what matters ultimately is your ability to be disciplined about sticking to the choices you make.
- Be sensitive to changing circumstances—important dates, milestones, life stages, new commitments and relationships, since all of these may require you to re-examine your choices, and what was good balance may no longer work with changed circumstances or new or changed people and commitments in your life.

9

The Shastra of Managing a Portfolio of Brands

Lessons in Creating True Diversity at Work

I WONDER WHY WE DON'T GET MORE OUT-OF-THE-BOX THINKING? WE DID INCREASE DIVERSITY BY GETTING ONE LEAD TEAM MEMBER WHO DOESN'T PLAY GOLF.

So far we have focused on what marketers need to do to get their brands to succeed with consumers. However, there is something which marketers need to confront which is perhaps even more challenging than getting a single brand up and running. That challenge involves managing a portfolio of more than one brand.

One of the well-known milestones in marketing history was the introduction of the concept of brand management in the 1930s. Procter & Gamble pioneered this trend and then other consumer product companies rapidly followed suit. Simply put, the concept of brand management suggested that each brand was to be treated as an independent business entity, even a separate company with its own profit and loss statement, so much so that these brands were competing externally as well as internally. The model worked wonderfully for a long time, until people realized that a more strategic approach was needed to manage a portfolio of brands. This realization was prompted by changing retail realities and by the increase in competitive clutter. For example, marketers found that in some cases, different brands of the same company were trading users. This led to no increase in the overall sales of the company.

With the growth of large retailers and their greater bargaining power, the focus shifted from just growing a particular brand's sales to ideas that would grow the entire category. This change was driven by the recognition that companies make more money only if the total pie grows, not just by shifting volumes from one brand to another.

So 'category management' became the new buzzword, and since then virtually every marketer has been walking the thin line between driving a brand as an independent unit and adjusting for the greater good of the category. In many organizations which have more than one brand playing in the same category, mastering this can be critical. It can mean a big difference for overall company results. When a portfolio of brands is managed well, they can really work together to accelerate total company sales. On the other hand, when they are mismanaged, the result can be brands cannibalizing each other's sales and users, confusion for consumers and retailers and ultimately, far less than ideal results for the company. Over the years, marketers have learned some basic principles on how best to use a category of brands and I'll be sharing them below, taking an example from an iconic Indian brand which over time has extended its portfolio to a series of sub-brands, which all work together as a portfolio. This is the Taj group of hotels.

The first principle is to have a clear reason for the existence of each brand, ideally based on the consumer group it targets. Historically, many brands were positioned on their features (for example, a phone manufacturer talking about how they have both Windows and Android devices), but as we've learned in the earlier chapters, only when a brand is really differentiated does it stand a chance of success. The best way of setting up a brand for differentiation is to appeal to a different group of consumers. The Taj hotel chain has been an iconic brand in India since it was launched in

1903. This brand has been seen as symbolizing not just the ultimate in luxury and indulgence, but also to an extent a concrete symbol of national pride. One of the reasons for the latter is the backstory of how the Taj group of hotels began. Supposedly Jamsetji Tata was refused entry into a luxury hotel on the grounds that only Europeans were allowed. He then started the first iconic Taj Mahal Palace Hotel in Mumbai which faces the Gateway of India. The Taj group has since expanded overseas as well, with several iconic properties around the world, from New York to London to the Maldives. The way this iconic company has managed its portfolio in India holds some great lessons in managing a portfolio of brands. Over time, to cater to a broader base of potential consumers and keep their leadership position given the entry of many new hotel chains, the group has expanded the Taj brand to two more 'sub-brands'—Vivanta and Gateway. These two brands are designed to target the growing middle class, which cannot afford to stay at luxury properties of the group, and it's fascinating to see the clarity with which they are targeted. Vivanta is 15 to 20 per cent cheaper than the Taj, but the difference is more fundamental than price. According to the Taj group, Vivanta is targeted at a younger consumer than the flagship Taj. In their words, 'The average Vivanta by Taj customer is slightly younger, believes in no boundary between work and play and is rationally exuberant. He is the kind of person, because he is so intensely consumed by work, who understands the relevance of relaxation and therefore the little details of life.'

Gateway, priced 15 to 20 per cent lower than Vivanta, is targeted at a younger consumer who is seeing his or her first taste of success, and is much more focused on work around the clock. You could think of them as three different people or the same person moving through life stages—at an early stage of career at a Gateway hotel, with some more years of experience and exposure at Vivanta, and when they've truly arrived and want nothing but the best, the Taj.

The second applicable marketing principle is that when you have a clear reason for the existence of each brand, you can differentiate between the features and offerings of the brands based on who they target. In an ideal world, what works for the consumers of one brand should not work for the consumers of another. By clearly demarcating the boundaries, you are truly using each brand to appeal to a different set of consumers. The Vivanta range has as many as 155 differences versus the Taj, defined by the consumer it caters to. There is a clear understanding of the differences in the consumer—a younger consumer who works hard and plays hard versus a slightly older consumer seeking luxury and indulgence. This leads to subtle but clear differences, for example, energy drinks and bars in the room versus a selection of premium nuts and sweet snacks; shorter treatment times at the spa versus a luxurious treatment, a Sony PlayStation in the room versus high-end audio and video systems. Also, the Taj consumer gets more of what they want—custom-made and customized service. The staff-to-guest ratio at the Taj is 1.75:1, while at Vivanta it is 1:1. This translates to much more individual attention at the Taj. The Gateway range, catering to an even younger consumer who's likely to be wired for work around the clock, may have fewer restaurants. Also, it will focus on all-day options for quick meals versus large, signature specialist restaurants. The Taj group has executed this differentiation really well. The difference in the hotel brands is not simply pricing, but fundamental differences in the overall offering, keeping in mind the consumer each is targeting, leading to very different choices among what each brand offers.

The final principle is to be clear on what success looks like for each brand. We already know that one has consciously to ensure not to fall in the trap of trying to do everything the same way with each brand. In the case of the Taj group, that means that hotels of different brands will be in different areas depending on where their consumer base is likely to be. They will not compete for the same pieces of real estate; the expectations on expansion and margins will be different. The role of Vivanta and Gateway is to get a broader base of consumers into the Taj fold. Hence the expansion plan will differ. While many more properties may open up under Vivanta and Gateway, the flagship Taj may not expand at such a rapid pace, though it will keep contributing healthy profits to the overall company given its higher pricing structure.

When the Taj group wanted to expand into the budget hotel sector, it realized that tapping into those consumers, with the services and pricing it entailed, was best done through a totally different brand. While no doubt using the Taj brand would have helped that segment in terms of seeming aspirational, there may have been the risk of the flagship premium Taj properties losing some of their sheen. So when Taj expanded into the budget sector with a chain of three-star hotels, it was a different brand altogether called Ginger, with no mention of the Taj brand, unlike Vivanta and Gateway. Again, this was a sign of how astute they have been in managing a portfolio of brands to target different consumers.

Many other businesses use similar principles to drive appeal for their brand among different groups of consumers. A classic example which has been in use for many years is how airlines seek to differentiate between business class and economy classes. Those who don't do it well, establish differentiation solely based on features (bigger seats, more food choices, entertainment options, etc.). However, those who do it well, do so based on who they are targeting. A fitting example would be that of Jet Airways on its international segments. Their website does not explicitly call out any such differentiation but the visuals for economy classes show families with kids and couples, and those for premiere classes show single passengers, often in business attire. The description for 'Première Class' calls out things which would be more relevant for the business traveller, such as laptop sockets and linking the added space not just to more comfort but to having a relaxed atmosphere for catching up on work.

• • •

All of us are used to managing portfolios, even if we have nothing to do with the world of business or marketing. A common example would be the way we invest our savings. As any banker would tell us, we need a diversified portfolio, with some funds parked in savings for immediate liquidity needs, some in fixed deposits for higher and more stable returns, and some in real estate for capital appreciation. Seasoned investors even figure in equity for potentially much higher returns, though with higher volatility.

Each of these ways of investing money yields very different profiles of return and risk. Each of us has a different financial outlook and risk appetite. So we allocate our savings in a way that makes sense for us. However, we are intuitively clear that a fixed deposit will give steady returns but never the possible upsides of a good bet placed on a stock. We would not expect the same returns, but then we know that we would not have the same risk profile as well. These are portfolio calls we all make in managing our finances, and in doing so, use similar thinking to what marketers do in terms of clearly differentiating the role of each option in our portfolio.

At work, we're also used to managing portfolios of a different sort—projects or businesses. In my day job, part of what I need to do is ensure that my business has the right business model and plan for different parts of the portfolio. Some of these portfolios may have relatively lower profitability but give high absolute sales. They need prudent support levels because while they will not generate huge profits, they contribute to sales and overall company scale. Others may be very fast growing and have high profitability, but are small in scale today—those need to be invested in and nurtured for the long-term. There may be others which may not have a very clear right to win a long-term plan—those need to be fixed or deprioritized.

At a broader national level also, our leaders make such calls, and those calls can have lasting and far-reaching consequences. The rallying cry of ushering in a Green Revolution in the late 1960s and 1970s brought in tremendous changes in Indian agriculture and the economy as a whole. After Independence, the first instinct of the government had been to drive heavy industry (with Nehru's emotive appeal of these being the 'temples of modern India'). This led to a surge in investment in heavy industry, and the creation of large organizations like SAIL, BHEL and others who played an important role in helping build the infrastructure to support newly independent India. The growing infrastructure embodied a very real role in bringing together what had begun as a fragmented collection of former kingdoms and principalities.

However, by 1961, India was staring widespread famine in the face, and the government realized that while building steel plants and roads was great, agriculture as part of the national portfolio needed a revamp. Otherwise there was a real risk of a social catastrophe. The government cut through some of the traditional bureaucratic hurdles and started a 'test market' in Punjab with new rice varieties and investment in irrigation and agrochemicals. A new rice breed, which was soon called 'Miracle Rice', was developed. This rice had ten times the yield of traditional varieties.

This timely choice of focusing on agriculture as part of our national portfolio at a critical time had a lasting impact. India's rice yield tripled by the mid-1990s, and India became a major rice exporter. Most importantly, millions of people were saved from starvation. To put that into perspective, the death of hundreds of thousands, if not millions of Indians due to famine was a regular occurrence before Independence. In just the Bengal Famine of 1942–43, an estimated 3,000,000 lost their lives. After Independence, the vagaries of the monsoons meant that the threat of famines did not go away. India faced a number of such threats in 1967, 1973, 1979 and 1987 in Bihar, Maharashtra, West Bengal, and Gujarat respectively. However, these did not materialize into famines due to government intervention.[1] In Bihar for example, 2353 people lost their lives in the 1967 famine, a far cry from the huge death tolls that were commonplace earlier.

By the 1990s and the new millennium, India chose to grasp at its talent base and cost leverage to drive focus on another sector, which today is proving to be a big growth driver—software and outsourcing services. As with the Green Revolution, a strategic focus on a particular sector as a part of our national portfolio has had a major impact.

In my personal life, I sometimes think of the portfolio aspect when I consider my writing. Sometimes I'm asked why I write across genres, and my answer is always the same.

Any writer taps into his own experiences and passions, and I am no different. So I try and bring out the different aspects of my life and the experiences I gather there in the genres I write in. Books like *Brand Shastra* tap into my day job in the corporate world. With a father and grandfather in the police, and a childhood spent among people in uniform or in the Intelligence Bureau, thrillers are a natural genre for me to enjoy writing. Also, I love reading about geopolitics and history, and that led me to the dystopian genre. Each genre taps into different areas of interest, slightly different skills and certainly different publishers and readers. If I were to write a business book the way I write a dystopian novel, some people may find it entertaining but most readers would probably be put off (zombies appearing in the middle of a discussion on branding would be cool, but perhaps not everyone's cup of tea). The way I approach it is to manage them like any portfolio—recognize what's common between them (my love of writing, the same core skills), but also what's different, and also realize that together, they make my writing journey more fulfilling than if I'd been focusing on only one genre.

•••

Now, let's take the thinking on managing a portfolio of brands to a very real issue facing us today. That issue is about the diversity, or more accurately, the struggle to achieve much better diversity, in our workplaces. The

most commonly understood issue around diversity is that
of gender diversity. Given the various societal and cultural
barriers around women's education and participation in the
workplace in India, it is not surprising that women have
struggled to find equal opportunities, not just to enter the
workforce, but get their due when they become a part of it.
One would think that things would be better in the private
sector, where presumably women have the qualifications to
compete on an equal footing. In this scenario, male bosses
and peers would perhaps be more open to and accepting of
diversity. According to data quoted in *Forbes* magazine that
unfortunately is really not the case. While many women do
get entry-level jobs and at junior levels, the gender ratio is
much more even, as they aspire to more senior positions, the
gender ratio is very uneven. In Indian companies, women
occupy only one in eight management-level jobs. At executive
levels, that number falls to one in twenty. Multinational
companies are a bit better off, but only slightly. In MNCs,
women occupy one in five management roles, and one in ten
executive roles.

Clearly this is an issue, yet the broader issue is not just
one of gender diversity, but acceptance and encouragement
of diversity as a whole. India has one of the youngest
demographic profiles in the world, with a median age of
around twenty-six years, compared to close to thirty-seven
years in the United States, over thirty-eight in Russia and
forty-four in Japan.[2] This means an ever-increasing number
of young people entering the workforce, and working for

senior management which has shown little real desire to accept diversity. This conclusion comes after one sees the low percentages of women in management roles, even in multinationals. The dissonance between a young, aspiring and connected youth with an 'old school' set of bosses also leads to an issue of a mismatch between what these younger employees want and what their organizations can offer them. There is a lot of data out there, and depending on what you choose to lay stock in, estimates are that by 2016, close to 60 per cent of the workforce will be what is called 'Gen Y'. People belonging to Gen Y were born in the 1980s and beyond. Again, while there is divergent data on the subject, some industry experts like Shiv Aggarwal, MD of ABC Consultants,[3] have been quoted as saying that attrition among this group is much higher than the norm. In an article published in the *Economic Times* in 2013, Mr Aggarwal said that attrition among these young employees is as high as up to 25 per cent, almost double the average rate at most organizations.

Both gender and generational discrimination have in common a root cause—managers tend to hire and promote people like themselves. In a study spanning 120 firms, Kellogg School of Management Professor Lauren Rivera found a pattern of what she called 'replicative hiring'.[4] In other words, employers tended to hire those who were not necessarily the best equipped or qualified for the job, but those whom they saw themselves sharing social experiences with. In other words, people they could see themselves sharing tastes, experiences, leisure pursuits and social markets with. When people talk about there being an 'old boys' club' at play in organizations that prevents more diversity, they are closer to the mark than they may think. And the operative words are both 'old' and 'boys', since the fact is that hiring managers and senior management in most firms are older and male. This means that those from a different gender and from a different generation with very different expectations and backgrounds may not find a level playing field.

To be fair, a lot of organizations are trying to solve this issue. However, those solutions are largely framed around avoiding a negative, which is avoiding people resigning and moving to other jobs. So there are organizations with more liberal views on working from home, more flexibility around career paths, more open and accessible workplaces— all trying to help keep a more diverse workforce engaged and employed. But what if the conversation were to change slightly? What if instead of focusing on lack of diversity and avoiding attrition, organizations were to focus on the tangible positives diversity brings? What if instead of seeing it as potential attrition, a more diverse workforce was seen as an asset? This view would look at a more 'diversified' portfolio of skills and ways of thinking to help grow the business and organization. In doing precisely this, let's explore what we could reapply from how marketers think about using a portfolio of brands to grow the business.

In this case the first principle is to be clear on why each part of the portfolio exists and adds value. In any organization, diversity fundamentally helps because people of different backgrounds bring in different points of view and ideas. This helps a company innovate and grow.

In the two examples we have talked about, it seems suicidal, if not downright stupid, for any firm in this space to even think twice about gender diversity. The majority of consumers and purchase decision-makers for consumer products, whether they are personal care products or household products, are women. Having more women in the organization is not just 'nice to do' from a gender diversity standpoint, but critical to having an organization's fingers on the pulse of their consumer. Instead of having middle-aged men sit through focus groups and try and divine what women want, isn't it more efficient to have more women on the team bringing in that intuition and insight? And it's not just the 'traditional' consumer goods space that could benefit from that. Internet penetration, smartphone penetration and social media penetration are all growing faster among women than among men in India.

So for an organization that wants to stay in touch with their emerging consumers, those who will increasingly matter in deciding their fortunes in the years to come, having more women in the workforce and in decision-making roles matters. It's the same with younger employees. A growing young population base also means a growing base of younger consumers. The fact that Internet penetration is growing faster among women than men also mirrors my belief that gender diversity will become even more important for the next generation. According to IAMAI-IMRB data quoted in the *Economic Times*,[5] Internet penetration among college-going students increased more than 60 per cent in 2014. So the first step for any organization that talks about diversity is for the conversation to change from diversity being something good to something that is critical to continued business success. Without more gender and generational diversity, an organization in India today runs the real risk of being out of touch with its consumers. This can only lead one way for the business—downhill.

A senior PepsiCo executive made the following statement in a global advertising conference recently, 'I am sick and tired as a client of sitting in agency meetings with a whole bunch of white straight males talking to me about how we are going to sell our brands that are bought 85 per cent by women,' he said. 'Innovation and disruption does not come from homogeneous groups of people.'

Moving on, the second principle is to differentiate between different parts of the portfolio where necessary. Let's focus on the younger workforce, often called 'millennials'. This term was coined because they were born in the 1980s and 1990s and joined the workforce after the new millennium. There are a lot of differences between millennials and the older generation and any employer wanting to maximize their contribution would have to be sensitive to them. PricewaterhouseCoopers did a survey in 2012 called 'Millennials at Work' across multiple countries and some of their findings were extremely telling. For starters, development on the job and work–life balance count more for them than financial rewards. When it came to benefits, they rated self-development first, followed by flexibility, and then financial incentives like bonuses. Many organizations still seek to reward all employees with cash bonuses and vouchers. Would it perhaps work better to motivate millennials by rewarding them with sabbaticals or executive education courses? The company could pay for these as a tangible reward and invest in them. Another key finding of this study is that millennials are, as might be expected, much more technology savvy than the older generation. Many of these young employees feel stifled by old ways of doing things. Perhaps the best thing leaders in organizations can do is not to impose old ways of doing things, but when it comes to leading changes in processes or the way things are done, pass those projects on to younger employees. They will feel more engaged, instead of being passive recipients of the way things have been done. They may also bring fresh thinking and solutions to the table. That takes courage, but instead of talking diversity, an organization that truly wants to foster diversity in thinking needs to understand and use the principles of differentiating between different parts of the 'portfolio' to get the most out of each employee. They should do this not as a quota to be filled, but as something that truly can help deliver better results.

The final principle is to understand what success looks like for different parts of the portfolio and not impose definitions of success from one part of the portfolio to another. Taking the example of the millennials further, their expectations from their career are very different from earlier generations. When my father began his career, the most aspirational path was to join the government and spend one's entire career there and retire with a pension. Later, by the time I was finishing college, opportunities in the private sector mushroomed. This happened because of the liberalization of the economy and entry of major multinationals and Indian private sector players across many industries. However, for many people, the mindset of long-term employment as a desired goal continued, and most reward and retention policies at organizations reinforced it. When most companies give stock options, they come with long vesting periods, and progress and performance is still measured in a very linear way—ratings, promotions, levels. What the 'Millennials at Work' study found was that millennials increasingly are less loyal and are not seeking to spend their whole career working in a small number of organizations. In 2008, the study showed that only 10 per cent of millennials expected to have more than six jobs in their career. By 2012, that number had almost tripled, to over 25 per cent. Millennials do however expect rapid progression, but less so in a linear fashion and more through flexibility and learning. So an HR manager reading this book would do well to see if reward systems for younger employees could focus more on the 'here and now', since what motivates a fifty-year-old looking to cash in on those stock options on retirement may not mean as much to a twenty-year-old starting out in their career. Secondly, organizations can also see how career paths could be created that offer more flexibility and lateral movement to meet the millennials' need for development and diverse experiences instead of having them do the same thing for years on end.

According to me, the final point is the most telling. For all the 'newness' of thinking the millennials bring, their broader exposure and awareness of issues facing our world and society means that perhaps they are actually more conscious of the values of an organization. The old stereotype of the 'salary man' slaving away for the monthly cheque despite a painful boss and dodgy business practices will not work for these younger workers. The 'Millennials at Work' study showed more than half of them would be attracted to an employer whose CSR values matched their own and 56 per cent would consider leaving an employer whose values did not match theirs. So perhaps another way an organization can fully leverage the difference this part of 'diversity' can bring is to employ their energies and talents towards issues and projects that benefit the community as well.

Just a little thinking of what 'diversity' might really mean and taking another leaf out of the marketer's playbook in this regard can unlock a whole new way of thinking about this pressing issue. Perhaps we can banish thinking of tokenism and quotas and move towards a situation where organizations can truly wield the power of diverse talent for the greater good.

• • •

THE THREE MANTRAS OF THE SHASTRA
OF MANAGING A PORTFOLIO

- Be clear why each part of the portfolio exists. Whether that includes your investments, members of a team or hobbies you have, the clearer and more distinct the reason for each category being there, the more they can coexist and add value to you. If you have two hobbies which both meet your need for quiet time before bedtime by yourself, chances are they will end up competing for the same time, versus say one which taps into a very different time, for example exercise in the morning.

- Treat each part of your 'portfolio' the way it should be treated instead of applying a 'one size fits all' strategy. We've talked employees, but the same applies to kids at home. A child who is introverted and shy may well respond to different ways of giving feedback than one who is outgoing and extroverted.

- Success need not mean the same for every part of your 'portfolio'. To take forward the child analogy, just because one child of yours wants to become an engineer doesn't mean every single kid in the family needs to join IIT coaching classes.

10

The Shastra of
Business-to-Business Marketing

Lessons in Making 'Happily Ever After'
Stay That Way

SINCE HE'S ON THE NET SO MUCH, WISH I COULD
DOWNLOAD AN UPGRADE TO FATHER 1.0 INSTEAD
OF HUSBAND 1.0 HE CAME WITH.

A lot of the examples and lessons we've covered so far stem from the world of consumer marketing. Building brands and businesses in the sphere of consumer products (often called Fast Moving Consumer Goods, or FMCG in short) is where most of the principles of marketing first evolved, were perfected and then taught at business schools and through books. However, there is another parallel and no less fascinating aspect of marketing. This is the world of business-to-business (or in industry shorthand, B2B) marketing. Consumer marketing tends to dominate widespread discussion and awareness due to its greater visibility and appeal in popular culture. After all, every single one of us is a consumer, and all of us do household shopping, use consumer products and are influenced by their advertising. However, what may surprise you is just how big the B2B market is. Let's take the e-commerce industry, a sector which has been in the press recently for its explosive growth and potential. In 2014, according to a Walmart report,[1] the B2B e-commerce market in India was $300 billion. That sounds like a huge number. But truly to put just how big it is into perspective, in 2014–15, 90 per cent of the Indian e-commerce market was B2B, while only 10 per cent was B2C (business-to-consumer). Hence one may well argue that B2B is where most of the real action is. Whether you're finding a new vendor for an e-commerce firm, selling construction equipment to an engineering or real estate firm, or software to a company, there are some principles that all B2B marketers tap into to grow their businesses and brands.

I will come to what is unique about B2B marketing in a moment. First, let's start with the fact that a lot of what it takes to build a brand among consumers is equally applicable to the world of B2B marketing. You still need to offer something differentiated in a way that would be relevant for your target. You have to win at the relevant moments of truth (though where those occur may be different—an industry event or exhibition may be the first moment of truth instead of a supermarket shelf), and you also need to find ways of building loyalty. While the execution could differ, the broad principles and way of structuring the thinking are very similar. There are, however, some important success factors a B2B marketer needs to focus on, which may not be as relevant to someone marketing exclusively to consumers. These differences can sometimes lead to dramatically different performances for a company or brand depending on whether it is targeting consumers or other businesses. A recent example that comes to mind is the market presence of brands and operating systems used on smartphones or computers. In the consumer space of smartphones, the clear market leader of operating systems in India is Android. It is brought to life by brands like Samsung, Micromax, Karbonn, Lava and others. Microsoft, with its Windows system, did not even figure in the top five brands in 2014 when it came to consumer smartphones. However, when one looks at the B2B space of selling operating systems used by companies for their computers and systems used by their employees (such as email services), the picture is radically different. In this space, Microsoft is by far the dominant market leader. They have market share upwards of 75 per cent when it comes to email platforms. This radical difference is one example, and very starkly marks the difference in approach that's necessary when marketing to consumers or businesses.

So, what uniquely matters when it comes to B2B marketing?

The first is that to be successful in the B2B space, a brand needs to offer ongoing value, not just instant results. In the consumer products space, barriers to shifting brands are much lower. This is true especially in a market like India where small-sized trial packs are prevalent in many categories so that consumers can try out a new brand at a very low financial outlay or risk. Many consumers do 'flirt' with new brands in personal care products or phones when they are newly launched. However, it can be a very different story in the B2B space. For a company which has invested significant capital or resources in a software system, engineering solution, or a new set of machines, it is much harder and makes less sense to keep changing suppliers.

So any customer in the B2B space would want a supplier who not only meets their immediate needs but can grow with them, can help meet their medium- to long-term needs and whose solutions don't run the risk of not being upgraded or modified to meet changing requirements. Taking the office software example forward, Microsoft has built huge credibility over the years through constant updates to its software and operating systems so it can keep pace with the needs of its customers—whether it is building in features in programmes to enable more online collaboration and sharing, or making its offerings available on tablets and smartphones and so on. When it comes to even higher capital or investment, this ability of a supplier to grow and evolve with the customer's needs becomes even more critical.

Another good example is that of defence contracts. Here, investments on each aeroplane or tank run into millions of dollars. The item has to serve for many years, and the stakes are as high as they get—as lives are literally on the line. The recent Indian Air Force requirement for a next-generation fighter aircraft, for which the French won with the Dassault Rafale twin-engine fighter, hinged not just on performance and cost (which the leading contenders were shortlisted on) but on other factors related to long-term value creation, such as transfer of technology and manufacturing in India that would serve ongoing benefits to the Indian aviation industry. Another important factor was the parallel negotiations on upgrades to the Mirage 2000 fighters the IAF already had in service, also from the same company. The 'Make in India' push that Prime Minister Modi is driving with potential foreign suppliers and partners across industries is another way the government is trying to get more ongoing 'value' from potential suppliers. In other words, not just getting good quality and value items (fighter planes in this case) here and now, but getting technology transfer, manufacturing in India, which build ongoing benefits for India. While most B2B contracts don't take the number of years and protracted

negotiations that a major multibillion-dollar contract such as
this one did, the thought process a customer goes through
while choosing a supplier is not very different. Customers
will look at costs and quality at a particular point in time, but
also consider operating costs, upgrades, warranties, service
contracts and so on—all linked to long-term value.

The next principle is that to be truly successful, a B2B
marketer must be seen as a thought leader in the field. There
is a good reason pharmaceutical companies invite doctors for
conferences and beauty product suppliers call salon owners
to workshops. The big difference between marketing to
consumers and marketing to businesses is that in the latter
case, you are often marketing to those who are themselves
experts or practitioners in the field. So the value experts
ascribe to a potential supplier is not just the cost and product,
but also whether the supplier is seen as someone whose
knowledge of the field they can trust. Building this credibility
means that any future products, services and ongoing ideas
that a manufacturer or supplier brings to the table are seen
as being more credible. Any B2B marketer thus strives to be
seen as a thought leader in the field, not just abreast of the
latest trends in the industry, but ideally as someone being at
the cutting edge of those trends to offer solutions that offer
customers new ways of doing business. That way, the next
time you offer a system upgrade or a wholly new idea, you
can build off that equity you've established in the customers'
minds. Yes, building equity and differentiating work just as
well for institutional customers buying machine parts as they

do for consumers buying detergent. It's just that the way of building both equity and differentiation vary.

Now one of the most important aspects of being seen as a thought leader is to be seen as 'ahead of the curve', in other words, anticipating the future and preparing for it instead of reacting to events. Much has been written about the e-commerce boom and companies like Flipkart and Snapdeal dominating the share of mentions in the media due to their visibility and advertising. However, one of the biggest successes created by using technology in a space where it had not traditionally been used is the company Oyo Rooms. Created by Ritesh Agarwal, a twenty-one-year-old, Oyo Rooms brought a totally new business model to the space of hotels. What he brought to the party was true thought leadership—pitching to small hotel owners and operators the advantages of branding and standardization. An estimated 415 million Indians undertake trips each year, and for most of them finding affordable hotels with decent quality services and amenities can be a challenge. While the end consumer need is clear, the B2B challenge is to get small hotel owners to sign up to be a partner in this effort. Oyo Rooms offered small hotel operators the advantages of branding under its umbrella, driving awareness and traffic to them online, as well as standardized booking and service platforms. In return, these hotels had to sign up for a list of nearly thirty standardized quality and service measures (down to mattresses, TV-set size and quality, Wi-Fi etc.). It was a win-win: the consumer got the assurance of quality and small hotel owners got the advantage of getting more customers (and happier ones!). As I write this, Oyo Rooms currently offers 63,000 rooms across 5500 hotels in 170 cities.[2] To put that into perspective compared to well-known multinational players, Starwood-Marriott has 18,000 rooms and the Indian Hotels Company (Taj) has 14,500![3]

The final piece that can make or break a B2B business is helping the customer solve issues or problems—in other words, troubleshooting. Very few people will call up the company if their clothes do not turn up as white as they expected after using the new detergent they purchased. However, you can be sure there will be a lot of telephone calls and follow-ups when an office's email server crashes or a factory's machines stop working, clearly because these can mean that the customer's business could be severely impacted. Some people call it 'after-sales service', but it is so much more than that. What matters most to B2B customers is troubleshooting or the ability to come in and solve problems fast so that business can go on as usual, or indeed to be readily available to answer questions and doubts. A good example in the Indian context is how ICICI Bank positions itself in targeting small-business owners to bank with it. ICICI clearly sets itself up as the thought leader in the field. It partnered with the International Finance Corporation, a part of The World Bank, to create and run the SME Toolkit site, which offers an online resource centre to help small Indian businesses become globally competitive. So, at one stroke, they are not just acting as people trying to get your money in their kitty, but offering real resources like information on taxation, management, tenders etc. The website has got over 2 million page views till date and no doubt has helped cement ICICI's thought-leader reputation among others in the segment. However, what such an effort also does is to provide a portal for instant troubleshooting going far beyond FAQs, including downloadable forms, draft agreements, how to contact experts for advice and of course, the opportunity to instantly get in touch for questions or doubts. This is a great example of not just solving issues when they arise but providing a whole suite of services and resources that are easily available, anticipating questions and problems a customer might have.

• • •

There is one area of my life where I have had to understand and practise the skills of a B2B marketer, and that is writing. To be accurate, I used these specific principles when I was learning how to 'sell' my work to prospective publishers. A lot in this section is based on reflection with the benefit of hindsight, and many of these lessons are things I picked up only years into my writing career. As a writer you too are selling not first to an individual consumer (marketing to readers does come into the picture, but only after you've been able to sell your book to a publisher) but a business (the publishing house); they are interested in not just one transaction but an ongoing stream of work (from a commercial point of view);

and since they are making significant investments in sales
force capacity, costs of printing and marketing, the stakes
for them as a 'buyer' of the writer's work are pretty high as
are the costs of failure (most starkly when it comes to unsold
inventory of books which bookstores return to them, to be
sold at a huge discount or pulped).

The first principle of offering ongoing value matters a lot
to a publisher because once they invest in building awareness
around an author and a reader base, ideally they would
want to keep building business off this initial investment,
choosing writers who can build off their existing reader base
for future books, instead of having to seek out new writers
all the time. That said, any publisher would not want to back
writers who are 'one-book wonders'. This importance of
building a reader base is one area where my eclectic writing
tastes may have worked against me when I began my writing
career. Yes, writing across genres was fun for me and I was
lucky I got to work with some great publishers. But thinking
back, I didn't really build up one novel or theme in a way
to get a more consistent reader base or 'equity'. I constantly
juggled with different genres and kinds of subjects. But that
was all till the *Alice in Deadland* series. When I wrote the first
book I didn't plan on it being a series, but when I thought to
take it forward as a series, I immediately saw the advantages.
One, I got readers who joined me along the journey. That in
itself was intensely rewarding because through the Facebook
group for the book I got to know hundreds of them well.
They came up with ideas, inspired me to take the story

forward, and rooted for me—all the things a writer could want from his readers. Also, very importantly, publishers began to view this as a big advantage. While I am writing this book, the *Alice in Deadland* series is being published in Turkish, Portuguese, French and German, and every one of those publishers has signed up at least the first three books in the series. It's a win-win for us all. For me, in not having to worry about finding a 'home' for each book in isolation, and for these publishers who know that their 'business plan' for my writing is secure for at least the next three years. They also have a steady stream of work to put in front of their own customers (bookstores) and readers.

The second aspect of being a thought leader applies equally well to writing and marketing your work to publishers. When I was younger, and more idealistic or perhaps naive, I thought all I needed to do was pour my labour of love out onto paper and send it off to the publishers. My first real insights into how to pitch a book and influence a publisher's thinking came with working with Wiley & Sons on my first business book, *Brand Management 101*. My editor at Wiley told me that since I was working on a book on branding, could I think of how to brand my own book better? It was as if a lightbulb went off in my head, and since then there's been no looking back. Every proposal and idea I send out or discuss is now not just based on an idea in my head, but on proper research done on the gap in the market it may satisfy. I now carefully look at other books in the field and their topicality, and determine what may set my book apart.

Thinking of each book as a 'brand' in itself has encouraged me to apply many of the same principles I talked about earlier. It has helped me pitch my ideas to publishers not just as another story a writer came up with, but something that is backed by thinking on how it builds off trends or meets an unmet need. I'm consciously trying to influence the publisher's thinking on why to pick my book, and by implication why it will be good for their business—and that's something any B2B marketer needs to do as well.

Finally, coming to troubleshooting, the reality of bringing a book to life is that actually writing it is hardly the end of the process. In many ways, that's where the publishing process starts. After the writing comes the editing, cover design, production planning and last but not the least, the marketing. Over the years, I've realized that a publisher places value in a writer not just for the written words they have produced, but also how accessible and open they are to chip in with ideas and respond to feedback. Sometimes that sort of engagement can steer a book in a very different direction, and for the better. If a writer is humble and receptive enough to respond to issues or suggestions, the end product does come out more impressive. In the case of the very book you now hold in your hands, it began as an idea to reprint *Brand Management 101* in India, but when I met my editor, Lohit Jagwani, over coffee in Mumbai, we chatted about other ideas. He asked me what I enjoy about marketing, and I mentioned the fact that it's all about people and their varied behaviour. I added that so many of these principles can be applied to everyday life. He asked if I'd like to write a book on that theme, and before we knew it, I was in the middle of working on a totally new book. I'm so glad I took his suggestion and embarked on this journey. Such openness, flexibility and willingness to act on feedback to solve issues or act on new opportunities presented by the customer is something a B2B marketer needs to do all the time.

• • •

Now let's take the thinking that goes into building a strong B2B business or brand to a context so many of us have to deal with every day—building a relationship that lasts. Specifically, building a marriage that lasts. For most of us marriage is a commitment that we hope *will* last. This is a partnership where we don't 'change brands' often (or ever) and where a lot of investment (most of all, of the emotional sort) is involved. And it is certainly one situation where failure is a very painful and difficult choice even to contemplate. Consumer marketing may have given us some principles that went into understanding what makes for a compelling matrimonial ad, but when it comes to understanding what it takes to make a marriage stand the test of time, we may be better off seeking inspiration in the land of B2B marketing. I am certainly not an expert on the subject, though I do have my own personal experiences to go by. So instead of this being a lecture on how we could apply the principles of B2B marketing to make a marriage (or honestly any long-term relationship) work, let's treat this as a conversation, where I'll offer up some food for thought.

Marriage traditionally is considered to be the most sacrosanct of Indian social institutions. It is full of rituals and myth, built around it through decades of tradition. Social norms and popular culture also play a big part. Bollywood has done more than its share in creating stereotypes of the 'ideal' marriage. In our society, once the couple is married, when it comes to making the marriage last, there is the expectation that somehow the couple will figure it out even when differences can sometimes prove to be irreconcilable. There is also a lot of social stigma attached to failed marriages. Yet, the reality is that this institution is coming under increasing strain and pressure. On the face of it the divorce rate in India is low. In an article titled 'Indian Matchmakers Targeting Divorcees', published on the *BBC World* website,[4] it was cited that the divorce rate in India was thirteen in every 1000 marriages (compared to 500 in every 1000 marriages in the United States, for example). However, this need not mean that marriages are necessarily happier in India. Social compulsions and stigma also force couples to stay on in unhappy marriages. To give a simple indication of that, while the Indian divorce rate is low compared to some other countries, in the country's metropolitan areas it is fast increasing, usually because with higher levels of education, emancipation and more nuclear families (with lower levels of pressure from extended families), partners feel less compelled to stay in a marriage that is clearly not working out. The same article cited that the number of divorces granted by family courts increased by 350 per cent in Kolkata between 2003 and 2011 and more than doubled in Mumbai in just four years between 2010 and 2014. It certainly looks like people could do with some help on how to make marriages work. Since I can't presume to speak for what a woman could do in a relationship, let me take this forward from a man's perspective—though I hope many of the women among you may find some of the learning applicable.

Let's take the first principle of B2B marketing again, that of ongoing value. In the context of a marriage it is one thing to feel attraction for another person and be together, and another to keep this attraction alive for the long haul. For too many people the reality of painful relatives, work stresses, kids and parenting, managing household chores and other realities of life override the initial passion. In such cases the honeymoon period quickly starts giving way to ennui. The clichés of 'keeping the romance alive' aside, what sometimes seems to make the most difference are the small things. In a study spanning 10,000 couples across 110 countries, bestselling author Fawn Weaver identified one of the key factors that led to a lasting marriage as the fact that successful couples maintained some rituals over the years, where they were able to keep doing some things all by themselves—in many ways, recreating that chemistry that brought them together in the first place. This could be simple things like having a coffee together each morning or having dinner together every day. To put it in Weaver's words, it is 'something that is just for the two of them and they maintain it every day. As with many other things in life, it's not the grand occasional gestures or gifts, but the little things we do every day that matter.'

And sometimes, these little things, rather than a one-off extravagant gift on an anniversary, matter much more in keeping romance and marriages alive. As Weaver concludes—'rituals enhance romance'. In finding these rituals that can be shared just between the couple, and having the mindfulness and discipline to keep up with them, can make all the difference. To go back to another example we looked at earlier, marriages, like any other relationship, require positive reinforcement. The more frequent that is, the more the desired behaviour will be achieved. In this case finding opportunities to be together is a form of that positive reinforcement. Whatever works for you, find it, and see if you can stick to it every day. See if that helps build that 'ongoing value' for you in your relationship.

The second principle of thought leadership is just as applicable to keeping a marriage going as it is to keeping a customer loyal to you. Just as industries evolve, our lives evolve and change. We move jobs, we move homes, we have children, we make new friends—the list goes on and on. But the common theme among marriages is that from the time a couple decides to get married, their lives will change and each change will bring its own challenges. One of the things a husband can do to help ensure that their marriage doesn't just survive but thrives is to be mindful of these changes and help lead the relationship through them. In many cases, husbands are 'blindsided' by the stresses and pressures that things like childbirth or a change in the home can bring to their partner or relationship. To take the United Kingdom as an example, research conducted by the charity One Plus One and quoted in a *Daily Mail* article[5] shows that the first year as parents represents the biggest threat to marriages. In the first year divorce rates were much higher than others. But don't despair. There is a way out. The Centre for Families, Work and Well-Being at the University of Guelph in Canada pulled together all available evidence on the subject in a paper titled 'The Effects of Father Involvement' in 2007.[6] The evidence, gathered from multiple studies around the world, was clear. When a father was highly involved in terms of spending time and attention preparing for the childbirth and also spending time with the child and spouse after childbirth, there were a lot of benefits for all involved. There were many positives for the child like better social and cognitive development, higher IQs, better economic success, ability to connect with people, and the list goes on. For fathers, it was feeling more self-confident, maturity in other interactions and more community participation. There was also a big demonstrated impact on marital relations with increased father involvement being positively correlated with a more stable marriage. This paper indicated that father involvement accounted for 25 per cent of the variance in midlife marital success. So, gentlemen, if you're married and are expecting a child, get involved. Read up about the changes that are in store for you and your spouse. Spend enough time with your spouse, do your bit to help out with the diaper changes and sleepless nights and most importantly, with the changes your life together will undergo. Take a leaf out of the B2B marketer's playbook and don't wait for the changes to happen and react. Be proactive in helping your wife through the change and lead your own thinking on how you will work through the changes. Start with some daily rituals where you can still keep some 'we time' for the two of you. Then move on to some chores you can help with. It's not just about winning short-term brownie points. By actually being more involved and helpful, your child and your marriage will be more successful and happy. The same principle holds for what one may assume are smaller changes like moving to a new city or country. Do your homework, anticipate what changes will occur, and be on top of them. Don't make your wife and family discover and deal with change by themselves.

The final point a successful B2B marketer needs to keep in mind is troubleshooting. That is just as relevant not only for a marriage but for any other relationship as well. Issues are inevitable in any relationship, but one must take the lead in solving them. When a customer brings up an issue, a good B2B marketer never gets defensive and explains it away, but takes the feedback into account and works to solve it. When the hotline buzzes with a quality complaint, the company doesn't blame the customer and tell them that there is something wrong with them. When there is a request for help, the company doesn't say it will get to it when it has time and is too busy to look into it now. Any such behaviour would lead to lost business and customers. And in a work setting you would say that is unprofessional behaviour. Maybe we should learn from the world of B2B marketing and bring that same sense of professionalism to our personal relationships. Which customer is more important to us than our partners, and what relationship is worth keeping more than the one we share at home? So, when you sense issues surfacing, or receive a request for help, drop that meeting at work or that night out with friends. Pitch in and see what support you can give and do your share of troubleshooting.

Now, am I painting the picture of a perfect husband, who is easy to visualize, but hard to be in real life? No, I'm just showing the behaviour that so many of us already exhibit at work each and every day. I am just trying to see what could happen if we bring that same mindfulness and desire to solve customer issues into our own homes. I certainly can't guarantee a fairy-tale marriage. However, chances are that applying some of these principles could help us ensure that a relationship that began with the initial feeling of attraction (or the perfect matrimonial ad) doesn't have a short shelf life, and that it continues to provide *acche din* to us and our partners for years to come.

• • •

THE THREE MANTRAS OF THE SHASTRA OF B2B MARKETING TO CREATE COMMITMENT

- Whether it is a relationship at work or at home, success doesn't end with getting the job, or getting married. It sustains when you can offer ongoing value to your partners, colleagues and employers. Whether it was that amazing first date with the one you would marry, or that job interview with the boss that sealed the job offer, try and keep that 'magic' alive over time.

- Help your partners in any relationship deal with the changes you and your relationship face, instead of leaving them to deal with it all alone. These change points (childbirth at home, a big crisis at work) are often 'moments of truth' for relationships and if you take an active lead in helping manage these changes, you strengthen your relationships and build commitment instead of allowing these changes to derail your relationships.

- Be open to feedback, instead of getting defensive. Don't wait for issues to bubble under the surface and blow up into a crisis. A good marketer, B2B or otherwise, spots issues early and acts on them.

11
The Shastra of International Marketing

How to Make the Most of Change in Your Life

REPORTS OF UFOS OVER MAJOR CITIES AROUND THE WORLD.

ALIEN INVASION

I HOPE THEY'VE READ THIS BOOK AND ARE LOOKING FOR ALLIES IN THEIR NEW HOME.

As consumers, one of the things that has changed over the last few decades is the extent to which we are exposed to, and marketed to, by global brands. These are brands which may have originated far away but have become an integral part of our daily routines. Iconic brands we have grown up with, like Vicks, Lifebuoy or Dettol, are as 'Indian' as they can be in terms of the loyalty they evoke among us as consumers. But they are all not 'Indian' brands in the sense that they are all owned by multinational companies. As we saw earlier in this book, marketers reaching out across oceans in search of markets and consumers is hardly a new phenomenon. Our ancestors in Harappa were branding their wares for sale in faraway Mesopotamia, and traders from other ancient civilizations were likewise setting sail in search of new prospects. Closer to our time, we can think of entities like the British East India Company as the true forerunners of the modern multinational company. This is because they may have begun as traders but quickly set up infrastructure to achieve a more lasting presence in the markets they dealt with. Today, of course, multinationals are all around us. As consumers, we sometimes don't really care which country a brand originates from as long as it meets our needs better than other alternatives. All the shastras we have covered so far are equally valid for any marketer trying to launch a brand into another market, or trying to grow his or her brand in a foreign market. You need to be differentiated, need to be successful at the moments of truth and so on, but there are some specific nuances that come with creating a success story in international marketing.

The first principle of being a successful international marketer is that you need to know where you can reapply what has worked for you in your home market and where you need to customize to win in a new market. If a Samsung or a Unilever were to start from scratch in every market with regard to their product design and strategy, chances are they would never be as successful as they have been in expanding across markets—Unilever for example, has its brands present in over 190 countries. Part of being a successful multinational company is that you take advantage of the scale of operations, range of capabilities and comprehensive knowledge that comes from being a large, global enterprise. Whether this entails R&D potential, design capability or marketing insights, being able to bank on dozens of years of experience across markets helps a multinational company gain critical advantages that it would never have had if each time it tried to invent everything from scratch. Hence Samsung broadly launches the same models in India as it does across the world, and also uses the same technology, branding and campaign strategy. Unilever too has many of the same iconic brands across various countries—brands like Dove or Axe are available in many countries with the same positioning and campaigns.

However, the truly successful multinationals don't just blindly launch what they have abroad. They take the time and effort to understand local consumers and adapt parent strategies where needed. Such flexibility and adaptability is often what sets apart the multinationals who thrive in new markets. If you think back to the 'Shastra of Differentiation' discussed in Chapter 2, most often adaptation is done where without it a point of parity would not be met in the new market. So, Samsung does not sell dual-SIM smartphones in most markets in South East Asia like Singapore, but in India many of its models have this feature. This is a well proven and understood expectation of the Indian consumer, many of whom use prepaid plans and dual SIMs give them flexibility to use different plans with better rates on data and voice. Also, frequent travellers use these to avoid roaming charges across states. To take another example, Unilever makes global brands like Dove and Clear available in India (and in other developing markets) in low-cash outlay sachets, which are smaller packs at affordable price points, displayed on hangers which can be hung up in the smaller kirana stores that dominate much of India. These sachets were introduced because without them Unilever could not penetrate into these small stores in India, and without penetrating these millions of stores which collectively make up a huge percentage of consumer product sales (often more than 90 per cent of category sales), a consumer products company cannot really hope to get scale in India.

The second principle most multinationals use when entering or exploring a new market is to find local allies who can help them. This is nothing new. If we think back to the Dutch and English traders who criss-crossed the world back in the sixteenth and seventeenth centuries in search of trade routes and fortunes, one of the first things they did on reaching a new shore was to find a local ruler or chieftain who was willing to become their ally. This local ruler or chieftain would help their foreign partners understand the lay of the land or gain easy access to authorities or markets. In more modern times multinationals do the same thing in many ways—some acquire a local company to get the capabilities and knowledge needed to win in the local market; others enter into a joint venture or partnership with a local company. Another way for many to acclimatize to new markets is to hire senior local talent who can help the organization understand the nuances of the local market. Few multinationals just fly in expats who run their business in India without any senior local talent or local partners. The same holds for Indian firms that are trying to expand abroad. With the growth of the Indian economy, increased liberalization and growing confidence of Indian firms, many businesses like Tata, Godrej and the Birla group are establishing footholds for themselves globally by expanding into markets across Asia, Africa and Europe. This qualifies these companies as true multinational firms, with operations, businesses, factories and employees across continents. A common route taken by these companies is to acquire capabilities aggressively by buying local companies or entering into joint ventures.

Between 2000 and 2007, the number of foreign acquisitions by Indian multinationals grew more than four-fold, and the value of these deals climbed more than five-fold. Many of these firms also invest in building up a pool of local talent with experience in the new markets they are going to operate in. Whichever route the company takes, what is inevitable for most multinationals is that over time, its face becomes more 'local'. This is important because local understanding and insight is what helps an international marketer understand how it needs to adapt its plans and strategies to succeed in a new market.

The final principle for most successful multinationals is that even as they adapt to a new market, they ensure that they retain the core elements of what makes the brand what it is. This is especially true in a globalized and connected world, where consumers increasingly connect with brands on Facebook and Instagram. Social media has no real limitations or physical national boundaries. It becomes very important to create a consistent brand experience and image for the globally connected consumer. So, while McDonald's has a McAloo Tikki burger in India and obviously doesn't sell beef products, the broad colours, design and core branding elements of the company remain the same. For example, a 'Happy Meal' is a 'Happy Meal' anywhere you go, though what's in the box may be different.

The same holds true for Starbucks. Its food menu is customized to the Indian palate—with paneer and more vegetarian options and so on. Many of the food items available in an Indian Starbucks would not be there in a store in the United States. However, the look of the store will remain the same in India as it does anywhere else in the world. This is because the experience of being in the cafe is a core part of the brand. Also, at the heart of the brand's product offerings, many of the items have identical branding and nomenclature. You could order a Venti Caramel Frappuccino the same way in Delhi or Dallas. What global brands do to achieve this balance between being standardized across the world while adapting their offerings to local markets is to understand what the 'heart' of the brand is. Getting this balance right is what really helps differentiate it over time among consumers.

• • •

The lessons an international marketer learns and uses resonate a lot with me in my personal life. The reason for that is a simple one. My father was in the government, so my childhood was one of constantly moving from one place to another as he assumed new postings. My life, both when I was growing up as a child and then as a professional, has been one of wandering, and frequently encountering new homes, cities, schools, workplaces, countries and cultures and learning to adapt to them. I was born in Nagaland, then lived in Kolkata, Sikkim, Delhi, Canada and then back to Delhi before moving to Ahmedabad to complete my education. As a result, by the time I finished my education, I had been to nine different schools across seven different cities. Once I began working, I was fortunate to have the opportunity to work and live in different countries as well. My years of growing up and working made me develop a love of travelling, and more importantly, not just being a tourist, but really immersing myself in the cultures of different places.

As I am writing this book, I have travelled to well over a 100 different cities around the world. I have either lived there, or travelled there on work or holiday. All of us are shaped by our experiences and this aspect of my life has had a profound influence on the kind of person I am.

Coming to the first principle outlined above, I've come to believe that deep down, we're all more similar than we'd like to think. In the course of my career, I've met consumers in over a dozen countries, ranging from in-home visits in rural Vietnam selling shampoo sachets to formulating marketing strategies for the premium skincare market sitting in air-conditioned malls in Orchard Road in Singapore. I've also had the good fortune to have worked with colleagues and partners of at least thirty different nationalities over my career. For all the superficial differences of language, race, colour, incomes and backgrounds, we are more similar than we might believe. Through this diversity of experience, I tend to conclude that we are bound together by values more fundamental than our shopping habits or SEC classifications. Those values lie in our shared desires to improve our lot and that of our families. This is a powerful driving force for me at work. I try and focus on not just selling more of what I am supposed to, but introspect, if in doing that, I am making a difference to the lives of consumers. Also, when it comes to managing an organization, I have come to define success as understanding what the improvement in one's lot means to each and every employee and try and help them achieve it.

Second, when it comes to finding 'allies', every couple of years as the 'new kid' in school, I learned very early on that you are always an 'outsider' to someone, and the key to fitting in is to let people know who you are beyond the labels they stick on you and also to get to know people beyond the superficial differences you may seem to have. When I first moved to Delhi at the age of five, I had no formal education in Hindi and became the 'kid from the Himalayas' (which I guess was first-grade shorthand for describing someone who had lived in Nagaland and Sikkim all their lives). Then we moved to Canada when I was nine, and I was the first Indian kid my classmates had studied with. I had to break the news gently to many of them that no, I didn't know Mowgli personally and my family did not own an elephant. Five years later, we were back in Delhi and this time I was the 'foreign-returned kid with a funny accent'. It just goes to show that being an 'outsider' or 'insider' is not an objective measure. When I listen to organizations talk about diversity, often I observe groups of people who consider themselves 'insiders' talk about bringing in more 'outsiders'. What's missing there is the realization that if you take a broad enough view of the world, we are all outsiders, or all insiders. It is up to us to define that in our own minds. My big learning from these experiences was to get to know at least a few people in the new environment very well to facilitate better understanding, beyond the differences. In short, I've gotten into the habit of always seeking out a couple of friends whenever I'm in a new environment and get their help to settle down and in turn, let them understand me better.

The final point is to understand what really matters to me and to define who I am. It was important not to lose this perspective despite all the changed environments I've found myself in. Moving around so much taught me two things—the importance of family, because when all else changes around you, your immediate family is your one real anchor and source of strength. Second, the fact that who you are can be and needs to be defined beyond where you happen to be studying or working. This is because your environment, workplace, designation or city can change, but every time your address or business card changes, you do not change as a person. Who you are needs to transcend these physical changes otherwise you will spend your life seeking validation in designations and labels others choose to stick on you. You will never really be the master of your own destiny. So my honest answer to the question of 'who do you work for' is that I work first for my family and then for the people whom I impact at work. Success for me is being the best father and husband to my family. It is to make the most positive difference I can to the lives of people at work. That goal, and that anchor, transcends which company I happen to work for, what designation I happen to have and indeed what I need to sell more of (and in which currency) at that point of time. My family anchors me in what's truly important to me, and helps me keep my perspective, when all else around me may change.

• • •

The broader applicability of the 'Shastra of International Marketing' extends beyond adjusting to new homes and workplaces. Under this there clearly are parallels to be drawn to the lessons international marketers use to thrive in new markets. The broader applicability comes from dealing with change in our lives, change caused by many possible reasons, but with one thing in common—the fact that we find ourselves dealing with people, situations and environments which are different from what we are used to. Research has long indicated that change is a major source of stress, for example, this could be moving houses, marriage or relationship breakdowns. Work-related factors, including unemployment and boredom, are also common causes of stress. In 1967, Holmes and Rahe came up with the idea of a 'social readjustment rating scale'.[1] Theirs was an attempt to quantify life change and find out which life changes had the biggest impact on an individual's stress levels. Below are the top five life changes identified as serious stressors:

1. Death of a spouse
2. Divorce
3. Marriage
4. Change in job/fired from job
5. Pregnancy

While some of these categories would be considered 'happy' changes such as marriage or pregnancy, this study revealed that change is the biggest cause of stress regardless of whether that change is 'happy' or not.

In the 1970s, Friedman and Rosenman carried out a nine-year study of 1000 people to find out if personality types affected stress levels.[2] They came up with the idea of the 'Type A' personality. The typical 'Type A' person is competitive, time-conscious and, overall, a 'workaholic'. I'm sure this description rings a bell and you know lots of people who could fit that bill, or perhaps you see a bit of yourself in that. You may well feel that being 'Type A' has its positives in terms of getting ahead in a competitive world. However, when it comes to dealing with change and stress, being 'Type A' has its disadvantages. Researchers have suggested that this sort of person would be likely to show more risky behaviour such as smoking, poor diet and so on when faced with stress due to change. In their study, 257 men died from heart attacks—70 per cent of whom had been judged as having 'Type A' personalities.

So, if change and all its attendant issues are a big cause of stress, what can we learn from international marketers to help us cope better with the changes in our life?

First, try and find the similarities between the changed circumstance you find yourself in and what was your comfort zone, instead of obsessing over the differences. Any of the changes mentioned above bring with them a change in routines, interactions and relationships. To ensure a smoother transition to the changed circumstances, do what the international marketer does. One simple tip is to continue some habits or rituals that you were used to before the change. I saw my own father deal with the death of my mother, and what kept him sane was continuing to write. Remember the importance of daily rituals we discussed in the 'Shastra of B2B Marketing'? A ritual of sitting down every day to write kept a sense of continuity in his life. This way he was able to keep his composure even while he struggled with loneliness and grieved the loss of his partner. You may not have such a traumatic change to deal with, but even if it's something simpler like adjusting to a new workplace or city, find some things you can do the same way you did in your old home or workplace. This way, even as many things change around you and need to be adapted to, you can feel in control of some things which are the same as they were in your old 'comfort zone'. This could be as simple as keeping up a fitness routine or a hobby such that during that morning run or when you're painting or playing music or tennis, you feel like you're in control because you're in an environment that is familiar and comfortable. Think of these hobbies or activities as refuelling stops, where you can retreat to when you're feeling intimidated by all the changes in your life.

As we discussed in the 'Shastra of Habit Change', without a conscious effort to deal with stress by injecting some positive habits or hobbies at those moments, you may perhaps pick up other coping behaviour like overeating or drinking too much. These will only have negative consequences.

Second, find allies to help cope with changes. Some of the major changes quoted above in Holmes and Rahe's study are negative (divorce, death). Certainly when you're facing any adverse change in your life, it always helps to have a shoulder to lean on, someone to confide in and to share your burdens with. However, even when the changes are not necessarily negative, it does help to have someone share the changed circumstances with you and to help you adapt to the changes. Pregnancy and childbirth are clear examples. We've already discussed in the 'Shastra of B2B Marketing' how studies have shown that the father being more involved during childbirth and helping to support the mother afterwards has benefits for all concerned, improving the relationship between the parents and the child's development as well.

Similarly, in the context of finding yourself in a new home or job, what you should be reapplying from the international marketer's playbook is to find your own 'ally' as soon as you can. A neighbour, someone who has also moved in recently, someone who comes from a similar background—basically, anyone who you think will empathize with you and with whom you can share the process of settling in. As I reflect back upon my own life and the major changes I have dealt with, both well and not as well as I could have, I can see clear parallels. An example of the latter was when my mother passed away. I did not seek out those I could confide in and share what was on my mind. This, despite the fact that I had some good friends around me. The bottled-up grief and frustration led me to drink too much and risk messing up my own health. That was till I met my wife, and began opening up and sharing what was on my mind. Gradually I got myself, and my health, back in shape both by having someone I could lean on and by picking up some new positive 'rituals' like running and writing every day to channel my energy in positive directions.

Third, don't lose who you are and what makes you tick, despite the changes around you. Just as a brand does not reinvent itself fundamentally when it launches in a new market but keeps its core elements intact, you need to keep your core values intact. With the life changes mentioned above, this means that even as you get married or have a child, don't totally lose your individuality. Keep some of those aspects of your personality and life consistent which are dear to you. Otherwise, all you will set yourself up for is resentment at some point in the future when you ask yourself if it was worth it to lose touch totally with the person you had been.

In the context of a move to another country or location, this means holding on to some traditions or roots that bind you to your origins and culture. This way, when trying too hard to fit in, you don't end up being rootless. If I take a personal example of how I bring this to the workplace, for me it translates into the core values and beliefs I have. No matter which company I work for, I would not be willing to compromise on those values. These values—for example, doing the right thing and not taking unethical shortcuts, of putting people first and not just focusing on short-term gains, of treating each and every employee with mutual respect— are fundamental to me. The flip side is that if I find an opportunity which is great on all other fronts (role, salary and so on) but suspect that there may be a compromise involved on these values, then I would not take up that opportunity. These are not just words. In my life, I have passed up some such opportunities that came my way because they would force me to change who I am as a person and the values I hold dear.

And that perhaps is the last and most important lesson that you could pick up from an international marketer. Some changes are thrust upon us—in the list above, certainly the death of a spouse or partner is not something we can control. But many of the changes are things which *are* in our control to some degree or the other, such as whether to marry or not; to take up a particular job or not, are decisions we can make, either alone, or in conjunction with those who are also going to be impacted by the decision. And the most fundamental choice an international marketer can make is that if entering or succeeding in a particular market means changing too much, to the extent that the brand is diluted or the brand's core proposition or values are compromised, then the marketer can make the choice not to enter the market at all. For example, Google decided not to operate in China given the conflicting views on freedom of expression and privacy. This is a great example of a major brand taking a stand and putting commercial implications aside. The company decided not to compromise on values that are important to it and chose not to operate in a major market. So, as you hopefully pick up some lessons from the international marketer on coping with change, the most fundamental lesson is to be mindful of what changes you embrace and what it means for you. The best way of coping with change is to anticipate it, prepare for it, and, if it does not make sense for you, then to exercise your choice of not embarking on that change in your life at that point in time.

Is that new job really only about the salary and designation or have you asked what it may mean for your daily routine, how you like to approach work, or the impact on your family? Would you get married just because 'it's time' or do you really want to think through what it means for your life after marriage? If you've been married for some time and are getting the gentle nudges from parents and relatives to 'start a family', have you thought through and prepared for all the life changes that a child will bring? Asking those questions will help you both decide on the change, if you have the option, and certainly prepare you for coping with it better.

• • •

THE THREE MANTRAS OF THE SHASTRA OF INTERNATIONAL MARKETING AND DEALING WITH CHANGE

- When dealing with any change, find the similarities instead of obsessing over the differences of your new situation or circumstance. Holding onto something that is familiar will help you feel more in control of some aspects of life even if many others change.

- Find your own allies and partners to help cope with change. Asking for help is perhaps the best thing you can do when faced with the stress of major change. Just as an international marketer looks for local partners to succeed in a new market, find your own allies (and remember to open up to those who are already there for you) as you face major changes, whether at work or at home.

- Be conscious of not changing your core even as change is upon you, and if you have a choice in the matter, be conscious of whether you want to embrace that change. Short-term gains from a change will at some point lead to resentment if you end up compromising on things that are fundamental to you.

12

The Shastra of Purpose-driven Marketing

Don't Just Transform Your Life, but That of Others As Well

SOMEONE'S GOT TO GET IT STARTED; MAY AS WELL BE YOU.

The final chapter of this book is not about the nuts and bolts of marketing, or about how marketers tackle a specific business or consumer challenge or how we can apply that in our daily lives. Instead it is about something much simpler, but perhaps much more fundamental. It is about an existential question that marketers and brands must importantly ask themselves. Those marketers that are already asking this question are starting to unleash much more powerful connections with their consumers and creating brands and businesses that are likely to truly stand the test of time.

That question is a simple one: Why do I exist?

If this sounds like philosophical puffery, the reality is that consumers are increasingly interested not just in what quality or value a brand or company offers, but also what impact that company has on the broader community it operates in. More so, marketers have to elaborate what their brand stands for in terms of the difference it can make in society. In industry lingo, this is called purpose-driven marketing or in the context of an overall company, Corporate Social Responsibility (CSR) efforts. However, in very basic terms, this means these marketers are trying to identify causes or issues they want their brand to help impact, and by making a broader positive contribution to society, create a stronger connection with their consumers.

In today's world, which is aware and connected through the Internet and social media, this broader impact to society matters much more. Several studies have shown that it's progressively not just about what business a company delivers, but how and why it does so as well. The extent to which this matters is evident from some data that was cited in an article titled 'Marketing 3.0 Will Be Won by Purpose-Driven, Social Brands' by Simon Mainwaring[1] in *Forbes* magazine. The story quoted We First, a global firm that trains corporations on making a positive social impact, which pulled together data from various studies to show this:

- Eighty-seven per cent of global consumers believe a business needs to place at least equal weight on society's interests as on business interests.
- Ninety per cent of global consumers would boycott a company if they learned of irresponsible business practices.
- Ninety-one per cent of global consumers would switch brands if a brand of similar price or quality supported a good cause.

So, if marketing is really about understanding consumers and delivering what they want, the above data points in a pretty clear direction. Brands and companies that want to win with consumers today need to pay heed to how they are seen as impacting the broader community they operate in. And if you're wondering if all this 'being good' translates in the bottom line, data quoted in that same article shows that companies that ascribe to such values (so-called 'Meaningful Brands') outperform the stock market by 120 per cent.

Given that marketing at its essence is about understanding and influencing human behaviour, brands and companies are uniquely placed to play a part in conversation about issues that matter and influence them. The above data shows that such engagement is increasingly no longer a matter of choice. Being good and being good for business are no longer contradictory. If anything, being perceived as good can help deliver better business results. Consequently, many marketers are focusing on the broader difference they can make to their consumers' lives and the communities they live in. To be totally honest, for some companies this takes the form of contributing money to some certified NGO to meet the statutory CSR requirements that the Companies Act 2013 stipulates. However, many brands and companies are going well beyond the basic requirements. In the process, they are not just making a big difference to the world around them, but also helping create a stronger brand in the minds of their consumers. To take just a couple of those examples that we've discussed in previous chapters, Procter & Gamble spearheaded efforts on providing clean drinking water to underprivileged consumers worldwide with its PUR technology, and Colgate used its leadership and reach in oral care to create better awareness of dental hygiene in rural areas.

Many other companies and brands can be added to this list. For example, Lifebuoy and Dettol drive awareness campaigns of better cleanliness and hygiene.

How do the marketers who are best at making this linkage between their businesses and broader social impact go about it?

First, they apply their brands and efforts to areas where they have an opportunity to make a real difference instead of just picking areas that are 'nice to do'. Every stereotypical beauty pageant contestant will mouth platitudes about world peace and eradicating poverty. However, brands and companies that really make a difference in purpose-driven marketing are those which apply what differentiates them and their brands to their particular purpose or cause. In other words, they play to what strengths they have as a company or brand in deciding which cause or purpose they support. A great example is Hindustan Unilever's Project Sunlight—or brightFuture—where the company is trying to impact the lives of children positively. Given the company's widespread brand portfolio across many diverse categories and its unparalleled reach in rural India, it is not restricting itself to just one area. Instead it is looking at several holistic areas such as food and nutrition (where brands like Knorr and Kissan can play a role), hygiene (where brands like Lifebuoy can play a leading role), building toilets (where Domex chips in), helping girls achieve their true potential (where Dove comes to the fore), and providing sustainable water to drink, wash and cook (where the company's Pureit water purifiers and range of laundry and household brands come in). Hindustan Unilever is a brilliant example of a company really trying to make a difference with a clear purpose by using the full set of strengths and competencies it as a company can bring to the table.

Second, these marketers do not do just one-off events, but create sustainable platforms that last and grow year after year. Just as successful brands are not built in a few months or even a year, creating a platform that will make a lasting difference to consumers and the community takes years to build and truly have an impact. Over time, some of these platforms become brands in their own right. Procter & Gamble in India has a programme called Shiksha, which has been running for many years. Just like Unilever's brightFuture, P&G's initiative brings together many of its brands around a common purpose—education for the underprivileged. Over time, Shiksha has become a brand in its own right, with advertising (with celebrity endorsers, no less), in-store displays and marketing plans which drive awareness for the cause and joins the company and its brand's commitment to it. It is a great example of a purpose-driven activity that has become intrinsically linked to the company and its brands over time—and not only is it good, but it is good for business as well.

Finally, all the companies and brands I've mentioned above do one thing to ensure that all purpose-driven activities are an integral part of the operations of the company, a part of its DNA, as it were—that is to solicit and sustain employee engagement of these programmes. In all these cases, these programmes are not run solely by a small central marketing group or a small group of senior management somewhere up in headquarters. A lot of the work is taken on by employee volunteers, who in addition to their 'day jobs' help out in these programmes. By doing so, employees take on their functional and leadership skills to make an impact to the community in addition to the business responsibilities they already have. In the chapter on diversity, we saw how among millennial employees, a match of values as per impact on community is a critical factor that determines their loyalty to an employer. So, on the one hand, fostering active employee engagement and leadership in such programmes is a great way to build commitment among them, but it is also a way to ensure that commitment to such programmes lasts through the years. This is because such initiatives do not hinge on a single leader or group of people driving it, but permeate the whole organization. Whether it's Project Sunlight or Shiksha, being involved in these programmes is something employees at these companies talk about with pride; and often, while their assignments or positions change to other divisions or categories, their association with these programmes continues over the years.

• • •

So what does purpose-driven marketing have to do with our day-to-day lives? Well, everything. Because, ultimately, how happy we are depends not just on our individual careers, love lives and families, but on the broader society and community we live in as well. I am sure at some point or the other, we have all thought of and spoken about things that are wrong with the 'system'. Poverty, income inequality, corruption, female infanticide, prejudices against women and communalism are some of many issues which society is grappling with. I'm sure you know someone who has raved and ranted about the things that are wrong with our society. And I'm sure you and I have done so at times as well. A brief glance at a typical day's Facebook feed or news headlines would bring into focus many issues that bother us. We often post about these online or support a cause by sharing something someone else has posted. At the very least, topics such as these certainly get more than their fair share of 'likes' and comments.

The big question is—other than commenting on these issues in the comfort of our homes, what are most of us doing about it?

The short answer is: not as much as we all could. And by that I don't mean any of you personally, but all of us collectively, as Indian citizens. While many of these issues require much more than an individual's contribution, in a country like ours where such a large number of people are not fortunate enough to have the opportunities and incomes many of us do, there certainly must be something we can do to give back to these underprivileged sections of society, right? Let's see how we're all doing on that front.

Since 2005, the Charities Aid Foundation has been publishing the World Giving Index, which ranks how charitable people across countries in the world are. This is based on interviews done in 135 countries by global research firm Gallup, and since its inception in 2005, there have been over a million interviews. So there is a considerable base of data across countries to help rank them over time in terms of how charitable or involved people in these countries are. The World Giving Index is based on the average of three measures of giving behaviour—the percentage of people who in a typical month donate money to charity, volunteer their time and, finally, help a stranger. So where does India fit into this report? Let the numbers do the talking:

	Overall Rank	Donate	Volunteer	Help Stranger
India (in per cent)	69	28	21	39

Less than one-third of us donate to a cause that matters to us, though over a third have helped a stranger in the last month. However, just about one in five actually volunteer to do anything to support a cause or issue that interests them. In isolation, these numbers don't mean much but the ranking does tell us where we stand as compared to other nations. As we can see, our country is ranked sixty-nine in the world in the overall index.

Who is ranked number one? The United States of America. I can immediately sense some of you thinking that these results must have to do with income, standards of living and money. When you have enough to eat and feed your family and can, on the whole, afford a better standard of living than a poorer nation like India, only then will you go out and help others, right? Surely, the numbers above must be pretty okay considering that we are still a developing country? Given the fact that the countries after the US on the list include Canada, Ireland, New Zealand and Australia, one may well start concluding this is indeed the case. That's till one considers the country that is tied in first place with the United States.

Myanmar.

Or the fact that there are many other countries which are also developing like ours and with social or political issues of their own where ordinary citizens seem to be doing more than us to help shape their community for the better. Sri Lanka is at rank nine, Bhutan at eleven, Kenya at fifteen, Nigeria at twenty-one. The list goes on, and the message is clear. Our status as a developing nation cannot be the only reason that explains why we as a nation are doing less to help each other, and indeed our economic status should be no barrier to doing so. Here are the rankings of some nations in Asia ranked ahead of India, to provide a basis for comparison to where India stands.

Country	Rank
Myanmar	1
Malaysia	7
Sri Lanka	9
Bhutan	11
Indonesia	13
Thailand	21
Philippines	30
Mongolia	32
Nepal	44
Taiwan	47
Korea	60
Pakistan	61

Given how competitive we tend to be in many spheres, whether it is aspiring to crack competitive exams, or in hounding our cricket team when they underperform, surely we can channel some of that competitive spirit to get higher on this list? If we were indeed to participate more in the community around us and help solve some of its issues, how could we go about it? The answers may lie in how some companies and brands mentioned above are going about purpose-driven brand building.

First, we should start by focusing on areas where we can make a real difference. When you talk to people who actually run NGOs, their biggest frustration is not that they don't get a lot of people who want to help out, rather that people drop out from volunteering very quickly after joining. This is because the initial enthusiasm doesn't last in the face of their other priorities and the fact that volunteering is hard work, much harder than sharing a post on Facebook. People typically stay motivated at something when they feel like they are adding value and making a difference. For most of us, that comes from doing things we enjoy or which play to our strengths or skills—in marketing terms, our points of difference. So what is your point of difference? The very fact that you're reading this book means that, if you're so inclined, you can help out in any venture that has to do with aiding the education of young kids in subjects like English or overall literacy, since you obviously would be educated enough to do so. However, helping and giving goes beyond helping the underprivileged.

To explain, let me take a couple of examples where I try and do my part in this regard. My writing career was founded on what I learned in the school of hard knocks (remember the many rejection slips?). So, one cause that's close to home for me is to help new, aspiring authors navigate the process and understand how it works. I also try and connect them to editors who might be interested in their work. No, it's not alleviating poverty, but helping young writers make their dreams of being published come true is pretty rewarding in its own right. Second, given my experience in the corporate sector, I am always open and willing to help out young entrepreneurs, especially those in the social sector or young graduates fresh out of college. In a more corporate setting, this is called pro bono work or mentoring. However, I would like to think of this more casually as chats, brainstorm sessions over cups of coffee where I nudge mentees in a certain direction. If you recall the chapter on turnarounds and how the odds seem to be stacked against entrepreneurs, helping even one of them beat the odds helps. In the context of my 'day job', I work for a global foods multinational, one with a rich heritage of 150 years of leadership in food and nutrition. So in India, it's natural that we focus on broad areas linked to our pedigree as a global foods company—hunger alleviation, nutrition, wellness, health, and finally education. No matter what you do, I'm sure there are areas where you can make a unique difference too. If you're a doctor, you can get involved in something to do with healthcare; if you have experience in communication, good causes always need to get the message out to attract funds. Whatever you do, you can help. Just think about your own 'points of difference' and see if you could tap into them to make a broader impact on our society.

Second, companies which are great at purpose-driven marketing build ongoing platforms or brands to sustain such efforts instead of meandering from one effort to the other. My wife, Puja, has an interest in working with kids, and that self-realization has seen her ally with causes over time where she can work with children. When we were in Singapore, she taught at a school for special-needs children and was a volunteer for the Make-A-Wish Foundation. While the specific cause and organization may differ, the focus is singular—kids who need help—and through these experiences she is deepening her passion for the cause and also building her own skills in the area. If she had started with teaching kids and then moved on to volunteer at an animal shelter and then something to do with vaccination, each experience may well have been very rewarding; however, she, and those whose lives she touches, would not have been impacted by the compounding effect that working in the same area over the years has brought for her. At the company I work for, while I would not say we have reached the scale of a Shiksha or a Project Sunlight, the intent is the same. Along with our partner, BAIF MITTRA (a pan-India NGO), since 2008, we have undertaken an ambitious programme of building sustainable livelihoods for the tribals in Akole Taluka, in the Ahmednagar district of Maharashtra. The programme currently covers thirteen villages and eleven schools and we have been steadily scaling up the impact on these families over time, including sharing expertise in nutrition, agriculture and education. In 2015, we instituted a scholarship programme to provide monetary assistance to five deserving girl students of these villages each year for pursuing higher education.

Finally, an organization that truly creates sustainable purpose-driven marketing makes these efforts something that involves everyone in the organization, so much so that it becomes part of the DNA of the organization. My organization partners with an NGO in Mumbai called Udaan, which ensures that underprivileged children get a strong and holistic educational foundation. Last year, our employees volunteered over 900 hours to support this programme, in addition to 100 hours spent teaching at the schools in Akole Taluka. When employees voluntarily spend weekends with underprivileged children and your employee awards each month are not just for sales targets but also for those who went out of their way to help the local community, then you know CSR is going beyond a marketing stunt. For us as individuals that can mean involving our family and friends in the causes we want to impact. When Puja began volunteering for Make-A-Wish, I would often tag along on wish-granting sessions. I would act as a Man Friday to take care of odd jobs. In one case I dressed up as Santa for a kid whose wish was to have a grand Christmas party. Puja and I were newly married then, and these shared experiences brought us even closer. So if you want to get involved in any cause, consider involving your family and friends as well. Far from being something that takes you away from your work and social commitments, whatever cause or area you want to impact then becomes even more fun and enriching. This happens because you're sharing it with those who matter most to you. It's also a great way to ground our children in the fact that they live in a society where every child is not so fortunate to have the kind of opportunities they do. Hence, they should help out where they can, thereby passing on the spirit of getting involved to the next generation. This is done not through exhortations or lectures, but in the most powerful way possible—by leading by example.

Yes, each of us in isolation cannot change all the things that are wrong with our society or help everyone who could use helping. However, every bit counts. In many ways, each one of us is a 'brand', and as this book has shown how many of the lessons that marketers apply to differentiating, creating and sustaining brands also apply to us in our day-to-day lives. But perhaps the most important lesson is the one contained in this chapter. The most iconic brands, the ones which truly live on in consumers' hearts and minds over the world and the years, are those brands which make a difference; which, if even in a small way, strive to create a better world. These are brands which have a clear purpose that drives them.

So, as we end our journey of exploring *Brand Shastra*, let me leave you with one final call to action. Take the learning from this book and see how you could apply it to your everyday life, but if you do nothing else, articulate your purpose: What your 'points of difference' are and how you can bring them to bear in your life, not just in building your 'brand' but in making a positive impact on those around you. You may well begin to transform your own life, but for sure you will make a difference to someone else's, and that is perhaps the more important transformation.

● ● ●

Notes

Chapter 3

1. Cohen, Heidi. 'Marketing: The 4 Moments of Truth'. 27 June 2013. *Actionable Marketing Guide*. http://heidicohen.com/marketing-the-4-moments-of-truth-chart/.
2. 'Shopper Decisions Made In-Store by Ogilvy Action'. 1999–2016. *WPP*. http://www.wpp.com/wpp/marketing/consumerinsights/shopper-decisions-made-instore/.
3. Whitler, Kimberly A. 'Why Word of Mouth is the Most Important Social Media'. 17 July 2014. *Forbes*. http://www.forbes.com/sites/kimberlywhitler/2014/07/17/why-word-of-mouth-marketing-is-the-most-important-social-media/.
4. 'Rahul Gandhi's Full Interview: First Text'. 27 January 2014. *Times of India*. http://timesofindia.indiatimes.com/india/Rahul-Gandhis-first-interview-Full-text/articleshow/29455665.cms.
5. Luthra, Pooja and Mala Jain. 'India's Performance Management Problem'. 3 May 2012. *Gallup Business Journal*. http://www.gallup.com/businessjournal/153278/india-performance-management-problem.aspx.

6. From Albert Mehrabian's official website: at http://www.
kaaj.com/psych/smorder.html. Also see: Mehrabian,
Albert. *Silent Messages: Implicit Communication of
Emotions and Attitudes*. Belmont, CA: Wadsworth, 1981.

Chapter 4

1. Customer Loyalty in Retail Banking'. 2010. Bain &
Company. http://www.bain.com/Images/Customer_
loyalty_in_retail_banking.pdf.
2. 'The Lowdown on Customer Loyalty Programmes: Which
Are the Most Effective and Why'. 6 September 2006.
Wharton, University of Pennsylvania. http://knowledge.
wharton.upenn.edu/article/the-lowdown-on-customer-
loyalty-programs-which-are-the-most-effective-and-why/.
3. Malhotra, Aditi. 'What Indian Parents Want Most for
Their Children'. 17 July 2015. *Wall Street Journal. http://*
blogs.wsj.com/indiarealtime/2015/07/17/what-indian-
parents-want-most-for-their-children/.

Chapter 5

1. Diamond, Dan. 'Just 8% of People Achieve Their New Year's
Resolutions. Here's How They Did It'. 1 January 2013. *Forbes.
http*://www.forbes.com/sites/dandiamond/2013/01/01/just-
8-of-people-achieve-their-new-years-resolutions-heres-
how-they-did-it/#3d02c049304c.

2. Stephens, Pippa. 'Binge Drinking "Link to Overeating"'. 24 April 2014. *BBC*. http://www.bbc.com/news/ health-27124357.

Chapter 6

1. Anjum, Bimal, Dhanda, Sukhwinder Kaur and Sumeet Nagra. 'Impact of Celebrity Endorsed Advertisements on Consumers'. October 2012. *Asia Pacific Journal of Marketing & Management Review*, 1:2. http:// indianresearchjournals.com/pdf/apjmmr/2012/ october/2.pdf.
2. Vaidyanathan, Rajini. 'India's Wedding Detectives Enjoy Booming Trade'. 11 November 2011. BBC World. http:// www.bbc.com/news/world-radio-and-tv-15520929.

Chapter 7

1. 'Samsung Beats Nokia to Emerge No. 1 in India: Report'. 20 August 2013. *Times of India*. Voice & Data Survey 2013, reported in http://timesofindia.indiatimes.com/ tech/tech-news/Samsung-beats-Nokia-to-emerge-No-1-in-India-Report/.

Chapter 8

1. Pahwa, Nikhil. '20 Charts on Advertising in India—Estimates for 2015'. 3 February 2015. Medianama.

http://www.medianama.com/2015/02/223-advertising-in-india/.

2. 'Flipkart Posted Rs 28 bn Revenue in 2014'. India Business Reports. http://www.indiabusinessreports.com/Blog/BlogDesc/89.

3. Furtado, Collin. 'Here's Why Rocket Internet's Foodpanda Exit Won't Reflect Struggling Indian e-Commerce Companies'. 29 January 2016. DNA India. http://www.dnaindia.com/money/report-here-s-why-rocket-internet-s-planned-exit-from-foodpanda-isn-t-entirely-indicative-of-struggling-indian-e-commerce-companies-2171562.

4. Boseley, Sarah. 'Working Longer Hours Increases Stroke Risk, Major Study Finds'. 20 August 2015. *Guardian*. http://www.theguardian.com/lifeandstyle/2015/aug/20/working-longer-hours-increases-stroke-risk.

Chapter 9

1. Drèze, Jean and Amartya Kumar Sen. *Hunger and Public Action, Studies in Development Economics*. New York: Clarendon Press, 1989.

2. Vorhauser-Smith, Sylvia. 'Tapping the Diversity of India's Talent Market'. 20 August 2012. *Forbes*. http://www.forbes.com/sites/sylviavorhausersmith/2012/08/20/tapping-the-diversity-of-indias-talent-market/#299db0253fb3.

3. Sengupta, Devina. 'Gen Y Demands: What Companies Are Doing to Keep Young Employees Happy and Motivated'. 12 July 2013 *Economic Times*. http://articles.economictimes.indiatimes.com/2013-07-12/news/40536569_1_gen-y-philips-india-yashwant-mahadik.

4. Rivera, Lauren A. 'Hiring as Cultural Matching: The Case of Elite Professional Firms'. *American Sociological Review*. http://www.asanet.org/journals/ASR/Dec12ASRFeature.pdf.

5. 'Women Driving Internet User Growth in Urban India'. 12 November 2014. *Economic Times*. http://articles.economictimes.indiatimes.com/2014-11-12/news/56025933_1_urban-india-june-2014-internet-user-growth.

Chapter 10

1. Fok, Evelyn. 'Start-ups Bet on Speedy Growth in B2B E-commerce Market'. 19 March 2015. *Economic Times*. http://articles.economictimes.indiatimes.com/2015-03-19/news/60286594_1_saif-partners-indiamart-bestprice-in.

2. Modi, Ajay. 'Oyo Goes Premium in Search of Profits'. 25 April 2016. *Business Standard*. http://www.business-standard.com/article/companies/oyo-goes-premium-in-search-of-profits-116042501215_1.html.

3. Bagaonkar, Swaraj. 'Indian Hotels Reboots By Going Asset-Light'. 30 March 2016. *Business Standard*. http://www.business-standard.com/article/companies/indian-hotels-reboots-by-going-asset-light-116033001103_1.html.

4. 'Indian Matchmakers Targeting Divorcees'. 11 May 2015. *BBC*. www.bbc.com/news/world-asia-india-32547360.

5. Lawrence, Julia. 'Sleepless Nights, Dwindling Libido and a Ruined Social Life: Children Can Wreck Your Marriage'. 20 July 2011. *Daily Mail*. http://www.dailymail.co.uk/femail/article-2016463/Sleepless-nights-dwindling-libido-ruined-social-life-Children-wreck-marriage.html.

6. Allen, Sarah and Kerry Daly. 'The Effects of Father Involvement: An Updated Research Summary of the Evidence'. May 2007. Father Involvement Research Alliance. http://www.fira.ca/cms/documents/29/Effects_of_Father_Involvement.pdf.

Chapter 11

1. McLeod, Saul. 'Stressful of Life Events'. 2010. Simply Psychology. http://www.simplypsychology.org/SRRS.html.

2. Friedman, Meyer and Ray H. Rosenman. *Type A Behaviour and Your Heart*. Fawcett Books, 1982.

Chapter 12

1. Mainwaring, Simon. 'Marketing 3.0 Will Be Won by Purpose-Driven, Social Brands'. 16 July 2016. *Forbes*. http://www.forbes.com/sites/simonmainwaring/2013/07/16/marketing-3-0-will-be-won-by-purpose-driven-social-brands-infographic/#6a883275156e.